TABOR EVANS

LONGARM

AND MAXIMILIAN'S GOLD

JOVE BOOKS, NEW YORK

LONGARM AND MAXIMILIAN'S GOLD

A Jove Book / published by arrangement with
the author

PRINTING HISTORY
Jove edition / October 2003

ISBN: 0-515-13624-7

A JOVE BOOK®
Jove Books are published by The Berkley Publishing Group,
a division of Penguin Group (USA) Inc.,
375 Hudson Street, New York, New York 10014.
JOVE and the "J" design
are trademarks belonging to Penguin Group (USA) Inc.

PRINTED IN THE UNITED STATES OF AMERICA

10 9 8 7 6 5 4 3 2 1

Chapter 1

"D'you know what we need in this place?"

"Another clerk," the U.S. marshal's clerk said.

"No, I'm serious."

"So am I," Henry said.

Deputy Marshal Custis Long gave Henry a dirty look. "Pay attention, son. I'm trying to make a point here."

"All right, Longarm. I'll bite. What do we need in this place?"

"We need a mirror. Nothing fancy, mind you. But we need a mirror so's a man can check himself over before he goes out. We represent the entire United States government when we walk out that door," he said, inclining his head in the direction of the door into the Federal Building hallway. "We need a mirror. Definitely."

Henry rolled his eyes.

Longarm felt of his chin. Smoothed his mustache ends. Fingered the hair that was beginning to surround his ears and curl on the back of his neck.

"If you're wondering do you need a haircut, Longarm, the answer is yes. You do."

"Do you really think so?"

"Yes, I really think so. Got a hot date tonight, do you?"

1

"What makes you think that?"

"If you have to ask . . ."

"I don't have any social engagements this evening," Longarm protested. Then he grinned. "But I'm told the lead singer in the new show over at Willard's is pretty spectacular. Great lungs, they say."

"Lungs?"

Longarm shrugged. He glanced down at his clothes and brushed some lint off the front of his coat.

"Custis, you aren't ever going to be pretty, if that's what you're wondering," Henry teased.

In truth, teasing though his tone was, U.S. Marshal Billy Vail's clerk was technically correct. The marshal's top deputy was far from pretty. Rather, he was a ruggedly handsome man standing well over six feet tall and with broad shoulders, a lean waist, and a born horseman's powerful thighs.

He wore light brown corduroy trousers, black stovepipe cavalry boots with flat walking heels, a calfskin vest, tan and white checked shirt, string tie, and brown tweed coat. The outfit was dominated, however, by the butt of a large and well-used .44 Colt double-action revolver carried in a cross-draw holster just to the left of his belt buckle.

His face was leathery from years of exposure to wind and weather. His hair was brown, as were his eyes. His mustache was a dark, abundant, but at the moment unwaxed handlebar.

"I wish t' hell I had time to stop at the barber's and then change clothes before the show," he grumbled, "but it's too far away, I'd never make it in time."

"Then go tomorrow night," Henry suggested.

Longarm gave him a dirty look.

"Sorry. I don't know what could've come over me to say a thing like that," said Henry.

"They're only gonna be in Denver for a short engagement," Longarm explained.

"And you musn't miss an opportunity, right?"

2

"Exactly." Longarm felt of the hair around his ears again. "You don't think I *really* need a haircut, do you, Henry?"

"Longarm, I already told you. Yes. You do."

Longarm sighed.

"But you aren't going to take time to get one, right?"

"Uh . . . right."

Henry shook his head and laughed.

Longarm failed to see any humor in the situation. He'd already gone and missed the first night. And they did say that Miss Stella Ingram had lungs that were, well, spectacular. There was no way he was going to miss being there this evening.

He pulled his Ingersol 1 from his vest pocket and checked the time. He could still make it. But there wasn't much time to waste. "Henry, if he doesn't want me any more today, d'you think . . . ?"

"Yes. Go on. If the boss comes out asking for you, I'll tell him you're off getting drunk."

"You're a big help to us all, Henry. I want you to know how very much us deputies appreciate you."

"And how much is that, Longarm?"

Longarm smiled. "On second thought, old hoss, you don't want to know."

"Get out of here, Custis. I'm sure he won't be looking for you this late in the day anyhow."

"If he does, lay a false trail. Tell him I've gone to light a candle in church. Tell him I'm visiting a sick relative in the hospital. Tell him I'll see him bright and early in the morning." Longarm winked. "Unless I get a better offer, that is."

Henry chuckled.

Longarm grabbed his flat-crowned brown Stetson off the rack beside Billy Vail's office door and headed for the hallway and Denver's Colfax Avenue beyond.

Yes, sir. They said she had great lungs. Longarm did intend to check that reputation out and make his own decisions.

• • •

The woman had great lungs. Stella Ingram was blond. And big. Not fat big. Just big big. As in tall. Statuesque. Long limbs, he presumed, although those were, of course, modestly hidden beneath the voluminous skirts of the several costumes she employed during the evening of entertainment. Handsome face with overlarge eyes, very wide mouth, although with lips a trifle thin, dark and striking eyebrows, prominent cheekbones, and well-defined jaw.

And of course those lungs. Magnificent. A man could feel quite good about climbing them, Longarm suspected. He probably would want to plant . . . something, likely not a flag . . . once he reached the summits.

Longarm spent the evening in fond anticipation of such an opportunity. He listened to the music, appreciated the songs, enjoyed the dancing. Why, he even got a chuckle or two out of the antics of the comic who made introductions and announcements between numbers. All in all it was a pleasant experience, made all the more so with the thoughts of what he hoped might come afterward.

When the final curtain came down and the attendants turned up the gaslights in the theater, Longarm stood and stretched away the tightness in his muscles brought on by several hours of inactivity, then made his way backstage.

He knew the way, and the staff at Willard's were well familiar with Deputy United States Marshal Custis Long. They only nodded to him as he went by, and if any of them thought to smirk and wink, he did not see.

Already there were several pale young men gathered outside the dressing room with a gold-painted star affixed to the door. Each of them carried a bouquet of some sort. Daisies or roses or the like. One rather plump fellow with slicked-back hair and spectacles had brought a crystal bowl of candies and sweetmeats that he hoped to present to Miss Ingram.

Bright of him, Longarm thought. At least if the lady

4

chose to spurn his offer, the boy would be able to eat them himself. The other swains would be stuck with useless flowers on their hands.

Longarm himself did not bother with such silliness. A raffish look and a twisted grin were all it generally took for him to attract the interest of an attractive lady.

Staying well back from the pack, he beckoned one of the stagehands over. "Do me the favor, would you, Bob?"

"Glad to, Custis."

Longarm had once done Bob a favor, a rather large one, which Bob had repaid many times over in this and other small ways. Bob pushed his way through the seven or eight breathless young men and rapped lightly on Miss Ingram's door. A moment later he slipped inside, then returned to view and motioned for Longarm to join him.

Longarm heard a few groans from the boys with the bouquets as he came forward and went inside the dressing room.

They would hang around a while long, he knew, and then begin drifting away in search of other, more receptive targets of opportunity. Likely several of them would end up this evening with young ladies from the chorus. Longarm would have been willing to bet that the boy with the candies would be the last to abandon Stella Ingram's door.

Longarm sauntered inside the dressing room with the air of a man who belonged there.

Then drew up short in mild surprise.

There was already someone in that room other than Miss Ingram, and he seemed to have brought a whole damned wagon load of roses and greenery . . . and champagne . . . along with him.

Bob gave Longarm a brief look of apology before he started in on the introductions.

Longarm only half-heard what Bob was saying, though. His attention was focused not so much on Stella Ingram as on the tall and—in his opinion—rather greasy-looking . . . but rich, no question about him being rich . . . fellow who was with her.

5

Chapter 2

"Mark Saint Sairy, this is Custis Long. Custis, this is Mark."

"Pardon." He pronounced it funny, Longarm thought. "But my name is not Mark. I am Jean-Claude Gilbert, the Marquis de Sant Cerre." He presumably was speaking to Bob, but looked at Longarm. Longarm likened the expression on the marquis's handsome face to that of someone who'd just spotted some dog shit on the toe of his boot. That seemed fair enough actually. Longarm felt pretty much the same way about the ol' marquis.

Who was, in fact, not at all elderly. He was probably in his early thirties, and stood as tall as Longarm. The marquis was lean and clean-shaven. He had slicked-back black hair and wore a tailored suit that probably cost Longarm's annual salary. There were ruffles at the cuffs and on the front of his shirt. Ruffles! And he smelled better than the damned flowers that filled the room nearly to overflowing. Longarm felt like puking.

Gilbert—he pronounced that funny too, like Jill-bear—was so damned handsome he looked artificial. Like he ought to be smoking a tailor-made cigarette on the cover

6

of some magazine or advertising cognac with a clipper ship pictured in the background.

"Pleasure t' meet ya, Mark," Longarm drawled, and stuck his hand out.

"My name, m'sieur, it is—"

"Hey, I gotcha, Mark. Like I say, it's a pleasure. An' I reckon you can call me Cuss if you're of a mind to."

"Cuss." Gilbert's lips thinned in what may have been a smile. Sort of. "How appropriate."

"Yeah, ain't it?" Longarm said innocently. He looked down at his hand, which Gilbert had chosen to ignore, then smiled and wiped his palm carefully on his trouser leg before turning his attention to Miss Ingram. He gave the lady his very best bow.

Before Longarm could speak, Gilbert interrupted. "But you must excuse us, monsieur. The lady and I were about to depart."

"But, Johnny, I—"

Gilbert ignored the lady's muttered protests—it seemed rather clear that departure hadn't been her intention at all—and turned his back on Longarm to offer his arm to Stella Ingram.

The woman with the more than ample bosoms looked once at Longarm, then twice at the massive array of flowers and champagne this smooth Frenchman had brought with him. With an apologetic little half smile and a suggestion of a shrug, Miss Ingram took the arm of the handsome Frenchie.

The Frenchie's won, Longarm ruefully acknowledged.

The lovely couple sashayed out into the backstage wings, leaving Longarm and his friend Bob behind with the flowers and the wine.

"Shallow bitch," Longarm mumbled as he started out.

Bob chuckled. "Sure, but aren't they all?"

• • •

Longarm got to bed early—unfortunately—and alone. He slept well enough and long enough that he should have felt in the pink come daybreak. In fact, he was still more than a little bit peeved. Asshole sonuvabitch Frenchie! Marquis indeed. Whatever the hell that was supposed to mean. The only thing Longarm knew about marquises— if that was the plural of marquis anyway; which was another thing he did not know—had to do with the Marquis of Queensbury, the fella who'd devised the rules for civilized contests of pugilism.

Now that marquis, unlike the dandy the night before, must have been a tough sonuvabitch to know so much about fisticuffs. Longarm figured he could respect a fellow like that Marquis of Queensbury.

But not the Marquis of Wherever-the-fuck.

Not that he cared. Not that he was still thinking about the asshole. No, sir. Not at all.

Longarm was scowling as he brushed first his hair and then his clothes—with different brushes, thank you—and got ready to go to work.

It was too early for a haircut and a shave. His barber would be open for business by now, but at this early hour there would already be a dozen or more men lined up waiting for their turn in the chair.

Longarm felt of the hair at the back of his neck and around his ears, and acknowledged that Henry had been right. He really did need a haircut. Needed a shave too. He fingered his chin and tried to gauge the stubble. It wasn't so awfully bad right now, but by evening he would look like a ruffian if he didn't soon have something done about it.

He pondered going to the trouble of shaving himself, and decided, mostly because of the haircut, that he would just slip away from the office during the day and pay that overdue visit to the barber.

With that settled, he buckled on his gunbelt, tucked his

watch into one vest pocket, and at the other end of his watch chain put his stubby little custom-made derringer into the pocket where a watch fob would normally be expected. The little gun had saved Longarm's ass more than once, and he would not have felt properly dressed without it.

As ready as he was likely to get, Longarm clattered down the boardinghouse stairs and stepped out into the cool morning air. Despite his previously gloomy mood, it looked like a perfect day was beginning, and Longarm felt increasingly chipper as he ambled across Cherry Creek toward downtown and the Federal Building, where the marshal's offices were housed next door to the U.S. Mint.

By the time he reached his favorite café, he felt so damn good that he made the wall-eyed waitress's day by flirting with her through his meal, then left her an outrageously large tip afterward.

This, he decided, was going to be one truly splendid day.

Chapter 3

"*Good* morning, Henry." Longarm punctuated the greeting by sailing his hat across the room to score a ringer on one of the hooklike arms of the coat rack beside the marshal's door. And if he'd been aiming at the top of the rack and not the hook, well, who knew that other than himself, right?

"I'm glad you made it in on time this morning," Henry said. "He said I'm to send you in the minute you get here."

"Something good?" Longarm asked.

"Oh, you're going to love this assignment."

"Henry, old fellow, I don't think I like the way you said that. What is it this time? Serving warrants? Some routine crap like that?"

"I wouldn't want to spoil the boss's fun, Longarm. But I can give you a hint if you like. This one is not what you'd call routine."

"Really? I think I like it already. Especially if it will get me out of Denver for a few days."

"Lucky for us all you're so easy to please," Henry said. "Go on now. He wants to brief you before the others arrive."

"Others?"

"He'll tell you." Henry inclined his head toward the door to the boss's private office. Longarm tapped lightly to announce himself before he entered.

United States Marshal William Vail—Billy to his deputies and his friends—was seated behind his desk with a reddish-brown folder open before him. He was in shirtsleeves, and gave the impression that he had been sitting there for quite some time despite the early hour.

The boss did not look at all like the rough-and-tumble Texas Ranger he used to be. His round face and balding pate gave him an air of cherubic innocence that he did not deserve.

There had been a time when he was as good a man in the field as there was in the business. Now he was just as highly respected in his role as a representative of the U.S. Justice Department's law-enforcement arm, perhaps largely because of the professionalism he brought to this politically appointed office.

Billy Vail played no favorites when it came to enforcing the laws of the land, and he demanded the same from his deputies. He was a good man to work for.

Now he looked up, saw who had come in without waiting for permission to enter, and motioned Longarm toward one of the chairs placed in front of Billy's wide, freshly polished desk.

"You wanted to see me, Boss?"

"First thing. I have a little work for you to do, Longarm."

"A 'little' work. Now that's just what I like, Boss. And the littler it is, the better I like it."

"Then this one should be a pleasure for you," Billy said. "It's mostly an escort thing."

"Mostly," Longarm repeated.

Billy shrugged. "Mostly escort, yes. With a little diplomacy thrown in."

"Diplomacy? Now wait just a dang minute here, Billy. If this is another of those deals where I have to spend two weeks smiling and taking tea with some senator's mistress, well, you can get yourself another boy. I've done my share of that an' then some."

"No, no. Nothing at all like that, Deputy Long." Longarm couldn't help but notice that the boss had reverted to a fairly formal form of address there. It was no more Longarm; now it was Deputy Long.

"I spent last evening with France's ambassador to the United States and his wife, Longarm. Lovely couple. They were with a deputy undersecretary to the Secretary of State."

"French?"

"No, the deputy undersecretary was ours. The only French official was the ambassador. But he was here on direct instruction from his government back in Paris. And the deputy undersecretary was with him on direct authority of the Secretary of State . . . ours, Longarm, not theirs . . . and he, I understand, is under instruction in this matter from the President of the United States. At the *personal* instruction of the President, if you take my meaning."

"In other words, this deal is plenty damn serious," Longarm suggested.

"Precisely," Billy agreed. "It is desired that our government perform a small service for the French government. And you, as a representative of our government, are the one being asked to get the job done."

"What kinda job, Billy? You say it's an escort, but I won't be playing nursemaid to any blue-haired old women, is that right?"

"Let me give you a little background first, Longarm." Billy leaned back and steepled his fingertips under his chin. "Some years ago, at approximately the same time our country was involved in, um, what one might call a

12

family brawl, our neighbor to the south was having troubles of its own."

"Mexico, you mean," Longarm said.

Billy nodded. "You may recall that at the time France saw an opportunity to reestablish a presence on the North American continent. Or thought they did."

"That was the thing with Napoleon and Maximilian, right?"

Again Billy nodded. "Not *the* Napoleon," he said. "A successor."

"Right. Not that I really know very much about it. I was busy elsewhere at the time."

"Yes. As a good many of us were," Billy said. "The fact remains, the French briefly occupied Mexico and established a puppet government there. They sent troops to support Maximilian against Benito Juarez and a number of other revolutionaries who opposed foreign rule of their country. And of course, eventually the Juaristas prevailed. The French were expelled with their tails between their legs, and without the muscle of French arms to prop him up, Maximilian's government collapsed and Maximilian himself was executed by the victors."

"All of which is ancient history," Longarm said, "so why should I care about any o' that now?"

"Personally, I don't care a fig more than you do, Longarm," Billy said, "but the French government cares, and they have prevailed upon our government to care right along with them."

"Fine. But how? Why?"

"During the conflict, Longarm, the French lent support to Maximilian in a number of ways, the military help being only one of them. They also provided cash to Maximilian. Lots of cash."

"Now it's starting to make sense," Longarm observed.

"Exactly. The French sent cash . . . gold, actually . . . so their surrogate emperor Maximilian could hire Mexicans to man his own army . . . much more politically palatable back home than the shedding of French blood if they could pay a bunch of barefoot *campesinos* to die for them . . . and arm and equip them."

"An army requires kinda a lot o' money, I would think," Longarm said.

"The French sent rather a lot," Billy affirmed.

"So why are we s'posed to care about this now?"

"Late in the conflict, shortly before the collapse of the French intervention, several shipments of gold were dispatched to French Guiana and on to Mexico City via Vera Cruz. The gold was sent in five . . . I suppose you might call them installments. There were five separate segments, each of those five being divided among three iron-banded chests and each of those chests containing one hundred twenty-five pounds of virtually pure gold bullion. Five separate segments, in other words, which each represented a total of three hundred seventy-five pounds of pure gold."

Longarm whistled.

"As you yourself said, Longarm, an army is an expensive thing to maintain."

"Was this gold lost or something?"

"You are on the right track. Of the five segments, three arrived safe in Mexico City. The fourth was intercepted by rebel forces not long after leaving Vera Cruz. The fifth and final segment was re-routed in an attempt to avoid capture.

"Knowing that the cat was out of the bag so far as the existence of the gold was concerned, the French personnel in charge of the shipment redirected those last three chests north to New Orleans, which was the only point in the United States that the colonel overseeing the shipment was familiar with.

"The gold was sent to New Orleans and then sent overland in an attempt to enter Mexico from the north and eventually get to Mexico City and Maximilian."

"All right. That makes sense. But I still don't understand where we come in," Longarm said.

"That final three hundred seventy-five pounds of gold never reached Mexico City. To this day, no one really knows what became of it. The French, accompanied by a detachment of Mexicans, are known to have left New Orleans with the gold loaded on three mules."

"Which is why the separation into smaller chests," Longarm guessed.

"Of course."

"Three hundred seventy-five pounds. And each pound is worth . . . lemme see. Thirty-two dollars an ounce. Sixteen ounces to the pound."

"Twelve," Billy corrected.

"What? Oh. Right. Gold is measured in troy ounces, twelve t' the pound. I forgot."

"The figure is impressive enough even at twelve ounces per pound," Billy said. "Don't bother doing the arithmetic. The total is almost $150,000."

"A man could throw himself one helluva drunk on that kind of money."

"True, but the French government naturally enough would like their gold back," Billy said.

"Why now? And why are they coming to us about it?"

"The gold has been assumed lost for all these years. Then recently . . . I don't have many details, but recently a handwritten account turned up in a bar in Marseilles."

"Where?"

"Some port in France." Billy shrugged. "The point is, a sort of treasure map was found along with an eyewitness account by a man who claimed to be a survivor of that failed attempt to take the gold to Maximilian."

"Hell Billy, I thought there was something interestin' here. Now you tell me it's just another treasure hunt. Have you suggested telling the French to go take a flying leap? They aren't gonna find any damn gold off some idiot's treasure map."

15

"Longarm, my friend, your opinion was not solicited, nor was mine. The President of the United States has said that we will assist the government of our friends the French by helping them find their missing gold."

"Jesus, Billy, this is nothing but a wild-goose chase."

"That may well be so, but it is the President's wish that you put on your goose-chasing clothes and give it your best shot. I think. . . ."

Billy's train of thought was interrupted by a discreet tap on his office door. Henry poked his head in and said, "Your guests are here now, sir."

"Very well. Give me one moment, please."

"Yes, sir." Henry withdrew, pulling the door closed behind him.

Billy retrieved his coat from the deer foot rack that hung on the wall near his desk. He pulled it on and buttoned it over his more than ample belly, then smoothed back what little hair he still had. "Get that other chair and put it over here with the others, would you, Custis? The ambassador is here, and, I presume, the man he has designated to represent the interests of France when the gold is recovered."

"Right, Boss." Longarm positioned the third chair quickly, then stood more or less at attention when Billy swung the office door open and ushered the Frenchies inside.

The ambassador was a distinguished-looking man with graying hair and muttonchop whiskers. He wore an actual scarlet sash across his chest and belly like a Sam Browne belt, and had a bunch of gaudy medals decorating his breast.

Longarm's attention, though, was on the man who accompanied the ambassador.

The other Frenchman was Jean-Claude Gilbert, the Marquis de Sant Cerre. It was the sonuvabitch himself, in person.

16

Chapter 4

"This is the man I was telling you about last night, Mr. Ambassador," Billy Vail said as the introductions were being made. "Both the President and the Secretary of State have asked us to give you only the best. Deputy Long is my top man. I can assure you he will devote his full attention to your situation for as long as your representative, the marquis, requires his services."

Longarm groaned inwardly. He was stuck with this bullshit treasure hunt. For as long as that popinjay Gilbert needed him.

If he'd had some inkling of what was to come, he might have been able to worm his way out of it. Play sick. Hell, play dead. Some-damn-thing. But now it was no longer between himself and Billy. Now the French ambassador had heard Billy's line of nonsense. Now the diplomat had seen for himself that Deputy Long was breathing and had no broken limbs. Dammit! Now it was too late to skee-daddle.

But . . . for as long as Gilbert needed him? So which of them was supposed to say just how long that was? Gilbert? Lordy!

Longarm gave the marquis a sidewards glance. If there

17

was any consolation, it was that Gilbert looked every bit as unhappy with this turn of events as Longarm was. And if Longarm's presence pissed the Frenchman off . . . that was to the good.

"Deputy Long is at your disposal, Mr. Ambassador. I'm sure he can be ready to leave within the hour if that is your wish," Billy was saying. He nattered on, completely oblivious to the dirty looks Longarm was giving him.

The two Frenchies began jabbering at each other in their barbaric language, and a minute or so later the ambassador informed Billy, "You may instruct your man to report to the marquis tomorrow at eight to receive instruction. At the Kramer House."

"Mr. Ambassador, you and the marquis should understand that Deputy Long's assignment is to escort and to assist. He is not, however, under the authority of any person or government other than our own."

Longarm felt like cheering. Good for Billy. Thank goodness for having a boss who understood what it was like in the field.

The ambassador bristled and looked like he was going to dispute that call, but whatever retort he was thinking of hung up on the tip of his tongue and remained there unspoken. After a moment he nodded. "But of course, monsieur."

Gilbert sniffed, much louder than could have been necessary, and gave Longarm a haughty look as if to say they would just see who was in charge.

Yeah, Longarm thought. They would for a damn-sure fact.

The Kramer House went past being exclusive. The place was practically secretive. They offered rooms—palatial suites really—but did not stoop to crass commercialism. Hell, they didn't even have a sign out front to show they were a hotel.

From the street the four-story Victorian structure looked more like a men's club than anything else. And in a manner of speaking, Longarm supposed they were a sort of club where only the wealthy and the well-connected would be welcomed.

The President stayed at the Kramer House when in Denver. Crown Prince Alexandre of Russia stayed there. Custis Long did not stay there or in places like it. He knew what it was and where it was only because deputy U.S. marshals were called upon now and then to aid the Secret Service in their function as bodyguards for extra-important personages. Longarm had spent several nights lurking in the shrubbery outside the Kramer House, but had never set foot inside the place.

Until now.

He ambled up the walk carrying his carpetbag in one hand and Winchester carbine in the other. The fellow who opened the door—he was dressed more like a butler than a doorman—looked positively scandalized to see someone approach with such scruffy luggage and a firearm.

"Sir. Please. I am sorry. Really. But the simple truth is that we are quite full. Filled entirely. We have no rooms to offer. Really." He nervously eyed the carbine as if he expected the nasty thing to blow up. "Really."

"Relax, neighbor. I'm here t' meet that French fella Gilbert." Longarm pronounced it the American way.

"Monsieur Gilbert"—the doorman pronounced it like the French did—"has not arisen, sir."

"That's all right. I'll wait for him."

Longarm squeezed past the horrified greeter and entered what looked to be a wide and very handsomely furnished parlor instead of a hotel lobby. There was no registration desk, but there were potted palms and plushly upholstered armchairs and Tiffany lamps with electrified light bulbs inside them. Electrified lights. Amazing. But he noticed there were gaslights too. Obviously they did not want to rely solely on the newfangled electric devices.

"Sir. Please. If you would care to wait, we have, um, you could wait on the terrace out back. Or in the garden. On the porch perhaps. Sir, about that . . . that weapon!" The poor soul looked really quite frightened.

"Thanks, chum, but I reckon I'll just camp out right here till Frenchie stirs his bones."

Longarm gave the man a cheery smile and plopped his rather disreputable-looking carpetbag—funny how he'd never particularly noticed how ragged it looked until this very moment—onto a very thick and expensive-looking Persian rug. He leaned the Winchester against it and dropped onto a nearby settee with his legs sprawled wide apart.

If that didn't get them to hustle the marquis down here, nothing would.

A portly gentleman wearing a diamond stickpin big enough to choke a goat came down the broad, curving staircase. He tried to pretend not to see the crass intruder as he passed through the lobby. The hell with that, Longarm thought. He tipped his hat to the gentleman and loudly said, "Howdy, neighbor. How you t'day?"

The gentleman guest grimaced and scurried out. The butler, doorman, whatever the hell he was, gave a barely audible squeal and dashed away.

Longarm figured ol' Jean-Claude would be down in no time at all. And so he was.

Chapter 5

"You embarrass me, m'sieu."

"Really? Now I'm real sorry about that, Mark m'lad."

"My name, m'sieu, is—"

"Are you ready t' go?" Longarm asked, ignoring the Frenchman's distress over his name being misunderstood.

Gilbert was standing between Longarm and the staircase, but he was not able to completely block Longarm's view. A woman wearing a dark cape with a voluminous cowl and hood came hurrying down the stairs and out through the back. Gilbert's distraction was not enough to keep Longarm from seeing that the woman leaving the Kramer House at this morning hour was Miss Stella Ingram, she of the pretty face and most excellent lungs.

"Is she any good?" Longarm asked.

"Pardon, m'sieu?"

"Stella. Is she a good fuck?"

"Sir! I am a gentleman. I know nothing of what you speak."

Longarm laughed. "Like hell you don't, Mark old boy. But never mind. That's water under the bridge. I asked are you ready to roll on outta here."

"M'sieu, I have not yet had my breakfast."

21

"You were s'posed to be ready to go at eight."

"I was . . . delayed."

"Yeah, and I reckon I know what the holdup was too."

"It would be uncivilized to depart without first enjoying a meal."

"That may be so, but your boss said we was to start the search where the"—he almost said gold, but realized in time that sometimes potted plants can have ears and the less that subject was mentioned the better—"the shipment was last seen. That'd be N' Orleans, right?"

Gilbert shrugged. *"Oui?* And so?"

"And so the only sensible way t' get to N'Orleans from here is first by train east t' the Missouri, then downriver by steamboat. An' the next train east leaves in forty-five minutes. The station is fifteen minutes away from here. So if you wanta leave today, you'd best shake a leg and get yourself moving. If you don't wanta do that, fine. I'll go tell my boss you've aborted the job an' ask him t' give me some other assignment."

"But, m'sieu. Without breakfast?"

It was Longarm's turn to shrug. "Your choice, Mark. We'll do this however you say."

Jean-Claude Gilbert looked like a thoroughly miserable man. But he recovered quickly, resigned to the loss of the meal. "Wait here, m'sieu."

Gilbert had a word with the dandified concierge, if that was what he was, and bounded swiftly up the stairs. Moments later, the concierge dispatched a flock of bellboys upstairs as well.

The whole crowd of them was back downstairs in five minutes or less, Gilbert leading the way and the bellboys trailing, burdened by enough bags, trunks, and bundles to outfit a traveling circus.

"I am ready, m'sieu. Lead forth," Gilbert announced.

Longarm was still staring in some disbelief at the amount of luggage the man intended to drag along.

"Surely, Mark, you can't be serious about taking all that shit with you."

"But, m'sieu. Every item is essential. Truly."

"You're crazy."

"And you are crude."

"We can't haul all that crap over half the damn country," Longarm protested.

"*We* will haul nothing. I, on the other hand, shall travel as a gentleman should. And this matter is ended. Shall we go?"

Shuddering and moaning, Longarm followed Gilbert and his army of bellboys outside. By some magic of the hotelier's art, the concierge had a carriage and driver already waiting there. The bellboys quickly loaded Gilbert's baggage—Longarm was surprised it all fit into one puny carriage—and bowed their way back into the hotel.

"M'sieu? You are ready?"

With a sigh, Longarm tossed his carpetbag onto the already overloaded rooftop luggage rack and climbed inside, Winchester in hand. He tapped on the small sliding window between the passenger compartment and the driving box, and told the driver to take him to the railroad station.

It took two porters and a four-wheeled hand truck to move all of Gilbert's luggage onto the train, and required that again a day and a half later to unload in Omaha. The man traveled with eleven trunks and cases. Longarm counted the damn things to satisfy himself that it was really so. And at that, he had trouble believing it.

"The Cattleman's Rest," Longarm told the driver of the cab in Omaha. All the luggage would not fit inside the hansom. The Frenchman had had to hire a second vehicle, a small wagon, to follow carrying the vest.

"*Non,*" Gilbert quickly put in. "We go to these Johnston House."

"Where the hell is that?" Longarm asked, his opinion of Gilbert unchanged after the many hours of silent association with the prick. "I always stay at the Cattleman's here. All us deputies do."

"Not this time, m'sieu." Gilbert handed the driver a coin—Longarm could not see what denomination it was, but it had the yellow glint of gold instead of the shine of silver—and repeated, "Johnston House, s'il vous plâit."

"Johnston House it is, mister," the cabbie said without another glance toward Longarm. The man climbed onto the box of his hansom, and the two-vehicle train rolled east, then south along the river for several miles until they reached what appeared to be a large private mansion.

"The Johnston House?" Longarm asked.

"Oui."

"Looks expensive. My vouchers aren't good but for so much, y'know."

Gilbert waved the concern away. "I pay. You provide escort."

"Well, I sure as hell don't understand a lick of this," Longarm said. "Not the least bit of it."

Gilbert ignored the comment, and sat stiffly on the rather grimy seat of the hansom when it turned into the long, poplar-lined driveway at the Johnson House.

They had traveled perhaps a hundred yards of the quarter-mile-long driveway when the cab rocked to a sudden halt and the driver shouted, "Don't shoot, boys, I ain't armed."

"What the—"

Two men had stepped out of the line of trees, one on either side of the driveway. Each held a shotgun in his hands.

"I got no strongbox, dammit," the driver was protesting. "This ain't nothing but a cab, mister. I don't carry valuables."

The holdup men wore masks, flour sacks with eyeholes

24

cut out so they could see. One of them had drawn a broad smile on the combed-cotton "face" of his mask. The one with the blank mask motioned with the barrels of his scattergun for the driver to dismount. Which the man did, practically throwing himself off the cab and scampering back toward the baggage wagon that sat a dozen or so paces behind the hansom.

The fellow with the grinning mask brandished his shotgun and stepped forward. Right where Longarm could see him out of the side window without any difficulty whatsoever.

"Fella out to know better'n to play with guns if he insists on being that stupid," Longarm said.

He raised his Colt above the level of the windowsill and shot the gunman square in the middle of his charcoal smile. That one dropped like he'd been poleaxed—which, in a manner of speaking, he had—and a bright red stain began spreading across the pale fabric of his flour sack.

Blank Mask was so startled by the unexpected gunfire that he jumped and accidentally triggered one barrel of his shotgun into the ground.

A swarm of lead pellets ricocheted off the ground, carrying bits of dirt and gravel with them, and the horses, probably stung on their feet and legs, bolted forward. The sudden acceleration threw Longarm and Gilbert to the back of the cab.

"Oh, shit," Longarm muttered. He snapped a shot out the window as the cab rocketed past the remaining gunman.

Blank Mask fired again, deliberately this time, but Longarm had no idea where that shot went, any more than he knew where his own bullet flew.

Gilbert yelped something in French, but Longarm had no time to bother with him. The damn cab was a runaway, and if the terrified horses weren't quickly brought under control, a wreck could do what those shotguns hadn't.

And Mama Long's little boy Custis had no desire to have the inscription on his tombstone read "Killed in a Runaway."

For that matter, he had no intention of needing either a tombstone or an epitaph. Not for quite a spell, he didn't.

"Shut up, Frenchie," he mumbled as he opened the cab door and began climbing onto the roof.

He could hear shouting behind him, but no more shooting, and in any event had no time for trivialities. Those people back there were on their own. Right now his concern was the runaway cab team. And staying alive.

Chapter 6

The cabbie had, thank goodness, wrapped the driving lines around the whipstock before he got down from the box. Longarm grabbed them and without taking the time to sort them out, simply hauled back with all his strength, dragging the horses down from their panic into a controlled run, and then in a sweeping circle out of the driveway and across a lumpy lawn toward the holdup scene.

"You'd best get down on the floor, Mark. Just in case," he shouted as the hansom bumped and clattered over terrain it was never built to handle.

When he got back to the luggage wagon and pulled the cab to a halt, all was calm. The cabbie and wagon driver were standing over the body of the hooded man Longarm had shot. There was no sign of the other gunman.

The cab driver hurried to take charge of his team, checking them over and clucking to them like a mother hen fussing over a pair of lost-now-found chicks. Longarm climbed down to the ground.

Inside the cab he could see Jean-Claude shove a small, nickel-plated revolver inside his coat. So, Longarm thought. The marquis might well be a fop. But he had fangs. There was no way to tell if he knew how to use them, of course.

Longarm ignored the Frenchman. If he wanted out of the cab, he was perfectly capable of opening the door and getting out on his own.

"What happened?" Longarm asked the wagon driver. Then he grinned and added, "After we left."

"This'un is dead. You c'n see that much."

Longarm decided not to say anything about that very obvious remark. Some witnesses just have to tell things in their own way, running their mouths for a spell before they get around to the point of things.

"The other'n, he shouted somethin'. I dunno what he said. It were in Spanish, I think."

More likely French, Longarm supposed, but there was no sense in questioning that either. Let the jittery fellow tell it however he pleased.

"Then a third fella wearin' one o' them flour sacks come outta the wood over there." He pointed. "That'un was leadin' three horses. He rode up quick an' the fella with the shotgun jumped up onta one o' the horses, an' the two o' them tore off fast as they could go back toward town."

Longarm grunted. "There were three horses?" he asked. "And the two men made no attempt to take their comrade with them?"

"D'you think I cain't count or somethin', mister? I said the fella come outta the wood leadin' *three* horses. He was riding one his own self, o' course. That makes four horses, d'you see what I'm saying."

"Sorry. I misunderstood," Longarm admitted. "So to begin with there were the three men, and they had a spare horse with them."

"Now you got it," the wagon driver said.

By then the cabbie had joined them, as had Jean-Claude Gilbert. "That's exactly right," the cab driver said.

28

Longarm grunted. He knelt on the hard, sunbaked ground beside the dead man and unceremoniously dragged the blood-soaked mask off him. The face that was revealed was that of a total stranger.

"Do you know this man?" Longarm asked. "Anybody?"

"No, mister."

"Not me."

Longarm was looking at Jean-Claude for an answer, though, not the local drivers. After a moment, the Frenchman realized that an answer was expected from him too. He shrugged and shook his head. "*Non*. Not I, m'sieu."

With distaste—like many who die violently, this shotgun-wielding idiot had crapped his britches in his death throes; the result was both messy and smelly—Longarm went through the dead man's pockets.

Whoever the man had been, he traveled mighty light. He carried a small penknife with two blades, part of a twist of chewing tobacco, and forty-eight cents in coin.

"Either this fella worked awful cheap, or he was expecting to be paid after the job was done," Longarm said.

"Monsieur, surely this was a robbery which you foiled, no?" Gilbert asked.

"No," Longarm said, "it was no robbery. They hadn't brought along an extra horse for no reason. An' unless one o' these fellas is important an' rich enough to be kidnap victims, it musta been you they intended to carry off with them."

Longarm was looking Gilbert square in the eye when he offered the suggestion, but Jean-Claude only shrugged once more. "We would not know, an' now we cannot ask, yes?"

"Yes," Longarm agreed. "Now we cannot ask." He stood and stayed there for a moment. The dead man, he saw, had spent considerable time in the saddle, and quite recently at that. His trousers were fairly new, barely beginning to fade from washing, yet the insides of the thighs were already worn shiny. And Longarm could see the scrape marks on his boots where spurs would normally be. He must have thought the spurs would get in his way today.

So where had he ridden from? And why?

"Got anything you want to tell me about this, Mark?" he asked.

"Non," Jean-Claude said. "I know nothing."

"How is it I find m'self to be a mite skeptical when I hear you say that? Never mind. Let's get on about our business."

Neither driver seemed reluctant to complete the terms of hire and get away from these two visitors. In fact, they seemed downright eager to get shut of Longarm and the marquis.

Chapter 7

Longarm didn't all that much mind being a bodyguard. Hell, it was a routine enough part of the job.

But he did not like the idea of being brought along to guard the body without ever being told that's what he was. If that was what the French wanted when they asked the U.S. government for an escort, why in hell didn't they say so?

What struck him as being even odd or was that Jean-Claude still would not talk about it now although the cat was out of the bag.

They registered—if that was what you would call it since the arrival was handled more like a visit than a hotel stay; Longarm never did see any money change hands— and Gilbert was whisked away to an upstairs room, leaving Longarm and his carpetbag alone in the lobby.

"This way, sir," he was invited by a distinguished-looking old man.

Longarm frowned and followed. But it would be damn-all difficult to guard Jean-Claude Gilbert if he didn't even know where the Frenchman's room was.

Rooms, Longarm amended once he saw his own down-stairs suite.

He had three of them. A bedroom, a parlor, and his very own bathing room with a bowl-shaped porcelain crapper and a water storage tank above it. A lion-footed bathtub sat on one side of the room, and there was a porcelain sink for shaving. Both the sink and the tub could be filled with water that flowed out of taps.

The elderly bellboy, if that was what he was, demonstrated how the taps worked. "All you need do when you want water," he said, "is to twist this handle. Here. You see? Water is always available. If you require hot water, pull the cord. Here. This cord out here"—he moved back into the parlor and pointed—"will summon someone if you need to have your clothing brushed or cleaned, if you desire a shave or a haircut."

Longarm still needed his hair trimmed. He hadn't had time before they left Denver. "How much is a haircut here?" he asked.

"There is no charge." The old man hesitated. "It is customary, however, to offer the young lady a tip. Five dollars is appropriate."

Longarm could feel his blood pressure rise. Five dollars? For a fucking *haircut*? That was scandalous. And the idea of having his hair cut by a woman . . . He shuddered. That wasn't natural. Didn't seem at all right.

"Would you like me to send the barber in, sir?"

"No," Longarm said quickly. "I reckon not."

"As you wish, sir. May I unpack for you?"

"No. That, uh, that'll be all."

The old man bowed. Paused. Finally turned and left. He was already gone before it occurred to Longarm that the fellow had been expecting a tip. Just for showing the way to the damn room. Huh! Probably wanted five dollars for that too.

Helluva place. But the rooms were nice. They were about as plush and handsome as Longarm ever saw, decorated with silk and brocade and tassels and shit. The furniture was fancy. And looked so flimsy he wasn't sure if he should sit on it. What would he do if he sat on a chair and it busted underneath him?

Helluva place. And this suite was likely inexpensive, or as close to that as the Johnston House came. If the hired help lived like this, there was no telling how large or how grand the marquis's suite of rooms would be. Lordy!

He shoved his carpetbag into the ornately carved mahogany wardrobe and propped the Winchester in there with it, then made sure his collar was buttoned and his shirttail tucked in.

He left the suite and rambled off in search of the dining hall. He was hungry.

Longarm did not see Jean-Claude Gilbert again for the next two days. He asked—repeatedly—for directions to the Frenchman's suite. Each time he was rebuffed, politely enough but firmly. He was not going to be taken to the marquis, nor did the Frenchie deign to come to him.

Great, Longarm thought. He was supposed to guard the son of a bitch, but didn't even know where he was.

For all Longarm knew, Gilbert might have slipped off somewhere and left his escort behind. Not that Longarm knew of any reason why Gilbert would do such a thing. But he could if he wanted to, and Longarm would be none the wiser.

Still, life was not entirely unpleasant at the Johnston House. He could make an appearance in the dining room at any time of day or night and be served pretty much any sort of food that struck his fancy. Steak, pork chops, eggs, oysters, fresh ocean fish brought in on ice daily, any damn thing.

In the smoking room afterward, he could enjoy his pick among the finest of cigars. Ask for just about any brand of any whiskey or brandy or wine. Be treated like a baron of industry.

Or a marquis of fine French lineage, he supposed.

Pretty much anything a gentleman could want seemed to be available at the Johnston House.

Including women. Sitting in the parlor, he was able to observe the comings and goings of the place, and from time to time that included the presence of some very handsome young women.

Longarm guessed one would be provided upon request. Just tell the old gent who had taken him to his suite, and a beauty would suddenly appear, available for his use.

That was a request Longarm had no desire to make. Oh, he was plenty horny enough. Much longer and he'd be looking for a knothole in the woodwork so he could pack it with grease and give it a go.

But somehow he just could not see himself approaching a stranger and asking the sonuvabitch to provide some pussy.

And even if he got past that and decided to do it, how the hell much would those girls charge?

It cost five dollars for a haircut here. How much more would it be if he wanted to plank the broad? Jesus!

It was there, though, if he wanted it. So was almost anything else, he supposed. The whole experience was something of a revelation. Not necessarily altogether a positive one.

The high living was not nearly distracting enough to make him forget that he was here for a purpose, and that purpose was being thwarted by Jean-Claude's continued absence.

Longarm was just short of storming the fucking Bastille and demanding to see Gilbert when at breakfast of the third day he was joined at his table by the marquis himself.

"You 'ave been comfortable, yes?"

Longarm grunted, and would have given the asshole a piece of his mind, but the marquis held a hand up to stop the flow of invective and said, "You will pack quickly, please. My things 'ave been sent on ahead. Our carriage waits even now. We must hurry to reach the *Pride of Kentucky* before she disembarks. Hurry now, please. They will wait for us, I think, but per'aps not so very long."

Gilbert smiled and left the table without taking a mouthful of food.

Son of a bitch! Longarm grumbled silently to himself.

But he helped himself to a solid breakfast of biscuits and sausage gravy while he complained.

He just wished to hell Billy had given this job to someone else. Anyone else.

Good gravy, though. He reached for some more.

Chapter 8

The *Pride of Kentucky* was as elegant a riverboat as any Longarm had ever seen, and a helluva lot bigger than most. It was a stern-wheeler which made it less maneuverable than the more common side-wheel steamers, but that allowed it to be built to a much larger scale than an ordinary riverboat.

Even Longarm's cabin was oversized, with room enough for two chairs and a small table in addition to the bed and wardrobe. The marquis had probably booked a suite for himself, Longarm figured. And if the boat didn't have suites included in the layout, Gilbert had probably hired several cabins and ripped out walls to make his own damn suite. The man did not make do without his comforts.

At least, though, there was no one who seemed interested in kidnaping him when they made the transfer into Omaha and onto the *Pride*.

Longarm stowed his gear, then ambled along the portside passageway to the salon, forward on the second deck. The lower deck held cabins, machinery spaces, and at the very front a covered—he didn't know what the hell to call it when afloat as sailors liked to use their own odd

36

jargon, but on shore he would have considered it to be a covered porch. There the cut-rate passengers milled about or squabbled over the few available deck chairs.

The second or middle deck held the salon, the gaming and dining rooms, and a galley.

The topmost of the three decks was open to the sky except for the wheelhouse and captain's quarters. Canvas awnings laced onto skeleton ironwork gave shelter from the elements for those who preferred to sit in the lounge chairs and watch the world glide past.

Something Longarm had noticed on other trips aboard riverboats was a sense of detachment. Whatever a man's cares, they were left on the wharf once he embarked onto the rolling brown waters of the big rivers. Aboard a river steamer, the steady splash of the paddles seemed almost to set the rhythm of a man's heartbeats. There was no need to rush or to anticipate, only to settle back and allow the boat and the river to carry one smoothly along.

It was a sensation Longarm found refreshing, as he did now when he climbed the stairway—called a ladder when on a boat, he was given to understand, and never mind that it was only a stairway and a rather narrow one at that—to the salon.

He enjoyed a glass of excellent rye whiskey and a slim cigar that had a pale and perfect outer leaf, then took his second whiskey back into the gaming room, where faro, roulette, and card tables could be found.

The Marquis de Sant Cerre was engaged in a friendly game of blackjack with some gents who looked spiffy enough that they might well have owned the boat. Or the odd railroad or two.

Longarm observed for a few minutes without being acknowledged by the Frenchman. He was not invited to join the game. Which was just as well. These boys were playing in a league too rich for him. They started a hand with a hundred-dollar ante, for crying out loud, and in the few minutes when Longarm watched, one pot reached a total in excess of two thousand dollars. No, sir, not for him, thank you. He took his whiskey and what remained of his cigar and searched out a poker table where the players lived in the real world and played for handfuls of silver instead of piles of gold and large-denomination currency.

"Deal me in," he said as he straddled an empty chair and dragged a few crumpled bills from his pocket.

An hour later and a dollar and a half lighter, Longarm thanked the gents he'd been playing with and went forward into the salon. He helped himself to another of the fine cigars and lighted it, then climbed onto the shaded top deck.

By then the afternoon heat was stifling, and there were only a handful of passengers taking what little air there was.

Apparently, there was a slight following breeze, and the speed of the wind subtracted from the movement of the boat left the air on deck almost in a dead calm. Smoke from the twin stacks amidship hung in the air, and quickly dissipated as it lifted toward the sky. A few birds wheeled overhead.

Among the passengers on deck were two women, one young and quite pretty, the other probably her mother. If it weren't for the old battle-ax with her, the young one might be worth an approach. Longarm was giving the matter some thought when a young, dark-haired man in a loose-fitting white waiter's jacket came to him and, once he had Longarm's attention, bowed.

"Señor."

"Yes, what is it?"

"Would you come with me, please?"

Longarm raised an eyebrow.

"There is a man, a gentleman, who wishes to speak with you. I do not know his name, señor."

"A gentleman, you say?"

"Yes, señor."

Gentleman was a word that could easily describe half the men on the boat. But the only one of them Longarm could think of who might have reason to summon him would be Jean-Claude Gilbert.

"Very well," he said.

"This way, señor."

The waiter took him downstairs all the way to the main deck, then aft along the passageway to another set of stairs—ladder if they insisted—that led to a very small and private observation deck on the stern end of the middle deck overlooking the broad, gleaming paddles.

From back there, the steady chuff of the steam engines and the hard impact as each paddle whacked the water and thrust powerfully into it was loud enough to make conversation difficult.

It would also be loud enough, Longarm realized, to prevent anyone from overhearing unless they were close enough to smell the speaker's breath.

There was no one else on the postage-stamp-sized deck. And no windows—would they be considered portholes on a riverboat; he didn't know—overlooked it from whatever cabin or cabins lay immediately forward. The little deck indeed offered an admirable degree of privacy.

Very nearly complete privacy at the moment, Longarm saw, because he seemed to be alone here except for the waiter.

"Where is the gentleman who wants to see me?" he asked.

The waiter only frowned, so he repeated the question, louder.

"Ah, yes, señor." The waiter smiled. "He is here."

The nice-looking young man reached under the front of his jacket and brought out an impressively large horse pistol.

Chapter 9

Longarm acted without conscious thought. The waiter, the smiling little son of a bitch, had instinctively stepped forward to make himself better heard, and they were standing virtually belly-to-belly when he pulled the gun.

Longarm grabbed the fellow's upper arms. Lifted. Twisted. Spun him to the side and pitched him over the rail, the unfired and as yet uncocked pistol still in his hand.

The man had one hell of a startled expression on his face.

The waiter's eyes were wide as he fell.

His mouth came open, but if he screamed, Longarm did not hear it over the pounding of the paddles and the thump of the engines.

The white-clad body fell, arms and legs scrambling for contact with something solid, onto one of the great paddle blades, the water sparkling bright in the afternoon sunshine.

Longarm winced as the waiter was quickly struck by the wooden blade, which churned the river's surface in thrusts powerful enough to send the huge steamboat racing over the water.

Something as fragile as one fairly small human body was of no consequence whatsoever to the massive paddle wheel. The man was quickly crushed and swept underneath the giant paddle wheel.

Longarm saw something protruding through the slim gap between the stern of the boat and the leading edge of the paddle . . . a foot perhaps or a hand . . . and for an instant he thought there was a scarlet tinge in the frothing water beneath the blades. But that might only have been his imagination.

He shuddered. Then took a deep breath and shrugged. Fuck the little sonuvabitch. He was dead. Longarm wasn't. Better that way than the alternative.

"I am busy. I will send for you when I have time, eh?"

"No, goddammit. We're gonna talk. In private or right here in the salon, I don't give a shit which, but we are gonna talk right now," Longarm insisted.

He did not look at the pretty young woman Gilbert had been engaged in puffing up with flattery—a rather phony and syrupy line in Longarm's opinion, although he did grudgingly concede that no pickup line was a bad one if it worked—nor offer to apologize to her for the crude language. Her aunt, on the other hand, the woman Longarm earlier had assumed to be her mother, gasped and gave him a look of prissy disapproval.

"You are being rude," the marquis said.

"You ain't seen rude yet. Now come with me for this talk or I'm getting off at the next landing and you an' your government can all go to hell. Without my help."

"Your orders—"

"My orders won't do you a damn bit of good if I decide t' go back to Denver an' tell my boss that I've quit the assignment. And why."

"But there is no need—"

"You want to talk about this here in front o' the ladies,

41

that's fine by me, friend." Longarm tipped his hat to the women and plunked himself down onto one of the sateen-covered salon chairs.

"You wanta talk first about the fella I had to kill last week . . . or the one I killed out there on deck a couple minutes ago?"

The aunt turned pale and looked like she was fixing to faint and topple over sideways.

Gilbert said to the ladies, "He is lying, of course. Being overly dramatic, *non*?"

"Non," Longarm said firmly. "We're one crew member short. The fella tried to shoot me. He failed, and now he's dead. And you and me are going to have us a heart-to-heart talk about all this, Jean-Claude."

"What, you no longer pretend to think my name is Mark?"

"You want an apology for that? Fine. I apologize. It was childish. I know what your fucking name is."

The aunt's eyes rolled back in her head, and the girl caught her and reached into her handbag for smelling salts.

"Now come along, Jean-Claude. We need to have that talk, and I'd really rather do it in private if you don't mind."

The Frenchman stood and made a leg toward the young woman and her fainting aunt. "Please to accept my most sincere of apology, ma'mselle, madame."

Longarm stood, scowling, and stalked out of the salon.

Gilbert took a moment more to fawn over the damned women, then followed.

Chapter 10

"Two men dead," Longarm said. "One kidnap attempt. One straight murder try. The kidnap aimed at you, the murder at me." He fixed Gilbert with a hard glare and demanded, "Why?"

The Frenchman shrugged. " 'ave no idea, m'sieur."

"Bullshit you don't." Longarm stood and stomped back and forth across the sitting room of the marquis's onboard suite.

As palaces went, this one was pretty small due to being confined by the size of the boat, but it tried to make up for that with the gaudy gilt and scarlet elegance of its appointments. Jean-Claude Gilbert had a fondness for the best, it seemed, and nothing less.

"Bullshit," Longarm repeated. He stopped. Whirled. Faced Gilbert again. "Bullshit."

"And what is the meaning, m'sieur, of this word of which you are so fond, eh?"

"You, Jean-Claude, are the walking definition of the term," Longarm declared. "You've lied to me. You and your pompous ass of an ambassador."

"His Excellency will not be pleased to learn of your opinion. He may choose to protest to your government.

43

He may demand apologies. He may demand your job, M'sieur Long."

"Bullshit," Longarm snarled. "An' don't try to change the subject on me. I don't care about the ambassador. I don't care very damn much about you. And right now I really don't much give a fuck about this job neither. I want to know what is going on here. I want to know why two men are dead. I want to know why I was told I was t' escort you when what you really need is a bodyguard. I want t' know where you and me are headed, and I want t' know why."

"But you have already been told the truth, m'sieur."

"Bullshit," Longarm said.

Gilbert shrugged. This time he sighed too. "What you 'ave been told is the truth, m'sieur, Perhaps not quite all the truth. But it is true about the gold shipment. Just as you and your marshal were informed. Every word of that is the truth. I swear this is so. That much is well known."

"So what is it that's *not* well known?" Longarm asked. "What part of this are you not tellin' me?"

"M'sieur, I have no answers for you. I 'ave been instructed to find this gold and to return it to its rightful owner, which is La Belle France. That is the truth."

"Jean-Claude, this story won't hold water. Your bucket has a hole in it. If it was just the damned money, you could reach into your pocket an' pay it. A hundred-fifty thousand dollars is a lot o' money, but you could pay that yourself and hardly notice it was gone. The way you spend, Jean-Claude, you prob'ly run through that much every six months or so anyhow. You could pay it. And that much money wouldn't be a drop in that leaky bucket for a government. And two minutes ago you yourself admitted I haven't been told the whole truth. So just what *is* this all about, Jean-Claude? What is the whole truth?"

"Officially, M'sieur Long, this mission is intended to recover the missing gold."

"An' unofficially?"

Gilbert shrugged. "If anything else should be found along with the chest containing the gold, I should recover that as well."

"Anything else?"

"That is all I was told, m'sieur. I am given to understand that certain documents were sent at the same time as the gold. It was assumed those documents were lost and presumed to be destroyed. The chance exists that they may still exist. If they do, it is my task to recover them and return with them to Paris."

"What about the gold then?"

"It would be good to recover that too, of course."

"But it ain't as important as these documents?"

"That is correct, yes."

"I don't s'pose you'd care t' tell me just what these papers are, Jean-Claude?"

"But m'sieur, I would be glad to tell you if only I knew. I was not given that information. It is not something that I need to know, you see."

"Y'know, Jean-Claude. I hate to overuse anything, even a word. But over an' over, the longer I'm around you, the word that keeps coming back t' mind just has to be 'bullshit.' It's the only thing that fits."

"I can understand how you would feel this way, m'sieur, but I tell you truthfully everything that I can. There was a chest of gold. It is missing. You and I together will recover it. And anything that we find with it. Your government and mine, they will be happy. If they are happy, you and I will be happy too, *non*?"

"If it was that simple, Jean-Claude, there wouldn't be men trying t' kidnap you or kill me."

"About that I know nothing, m'sieur. Truly."

Longarm didn't necessarily believe him. It was probably all just that much more bullshit. But for now it would have to do. One thing sure, though. Come the next opportunity to go ashore, Deputy Long intended to get a telegram off to Billy bringing the boss up to date on some of this stuff. Maybe Billy could get some answers out of the French from his end of things.

And Longarm would dearly love to have those answers so he might have some idea of what it was he was up against here.

He stood. "Go back t' your girlfriends, Jean-Claude. Sorry if I ruined your prospects there."

Gilbert smiled quite happily. "Oh, but m'sieur, to the contrary. You 'ave made the old woman upset. She should have a little something to calm her now, do you not think? Something to make her sleep through the afternoon, *non*?" He laughed heartily. "I think perhaps I shall be forced to see to the needs of the young thing while the old woman sleeps. So *non*, I must thank you for your help with this."

Longarm was shaking his head as he let himself out of the marquis's floating suite.

"No, sir," the *Pride of Kentucky*'s captain said, "whoever that man was, it wasn't any of my crew. I've had the purser check. Every one of our people is still aboard and accounted for."

"He was wearing a waiter's jacket," Longarm said. "That's why I assumed. . . ."

"Sure. I would've assumed the same thing," the captain told him. "But I can assure you he was not a member of this crew. He must have stolen the jacket. After all, it isn't like we've ever thought it would be necessary to lock them up. Who the hell would want to swipe a waiter's smock anyway?"

Other than a would-be assassin? Longarm couldn't think of anybody else either. But he would have liked to know who the dead "waiter" had been. It might have given him some thoughts on why if he'd had information on who.

"The boat is full," the captain went on, "but if you

would like me to arrange to have you moved to a different cabin . . . for your own safety, that is . . . ?"

"No, I reckon that won't be needed," Longarm told him. "For one thing, that one is cold meat by now. He won't be coming after anybody. An' if there are any more killers on board, I wouldn't want them making a mistake an' coming after some innocent soul you'd be moving into my cabin. No, thank you for the offer, but I reckon I'll stay where I am till we get to where we're going."

"As you prefer, Marshal. Naturally, if there is anything I or my crew can do to assist you, just let me know."

"Thank you, sir." Longarm left the wheelhouse and went forward to stand at the rail and peer down the wide, swift river toward far-distant New Orleans.

Hell, this job hadn't hardly started yet, wouldn't until they went ashore where the gold shipment was last known to be, and already there were two men dead. And one—himself—damn well confused.

The good thing, he reminded himself, was that he didn't really have to have the answers to all his questions. All he really was required to do was to keep the Marquis de Sant Cerre alive while Jean-Claude was doing the stuff his government wanted him to do.

That and to stay alive himself while he was at it.

Far behind him the paddles churned, driving them swiftly downriver.

Chapter 11

It was a meal to gladden any man's heart. Roast beef moist with the juices of its own fat. Mashed potatoes swimming in rich gravy. Biscuits light enough they needed to be heaped with sweet butter just to give them weight enough that they would stay on the platter. Coffee hot and fresh.

And a waitress pretty enough to make a man's blood run hot and randy.

The Frenchman hadn't appeared at the dinner seating. But then neither had the girl. Longarm could guess where the two of them would be.

Not that he was complaining. The black-haired little waitress was attentive to his needs, keeping his coffee cup topped up after practically every mouthful he took. And when the girl leaned over his shoulder to pour the coffee for him, he could feel the weight of her left tit warm on the side of his neck. The girl was short, but she had a build on her.

She stepped back from Longarm's side and crossed the room to fetch a tray bearing desserts. It gave him an opportunity to better look her over. He liked what he saw.

He guessed her age at twenty, give or take a couple

years. She had dark hair and large, dark, flashing eyes. Full lips. A very full bosom. Tiny waist encircled by a scrap of white apron over a very plain black dress. Funny, but the uniform did not make her seem the least bit plain.

When she returned with the tray, she once again leaned over him, the side of her breast soft against his ear. He wondered what she would do if he turned his head and . . .

Of course he could be misreading this whole thing. Maybe she was just angling for a generous tip from a well-heeled riverboat passenger. Not that Longarm had that kind of money, but he was traveling first class courtesy of the French government, and the girl would not know it was not his own money that was on display in his choice of stateroom.

Longarm shook his head to the selection of desserts. The girl did not withdraw at all, staying right there with her tit in gentle contact with Longarm's ear.

"Is there anything else I can get you?" she whispered. "Anything at all?"

Longarm tipped his head back and met her eyes. The pink tip of her tongue crept out from between those soft, full lips and slowly, provocatively licked back and forth. "*Anything?*" she repeated.

Hell, it was about as plain an offer as a man could receive.

He smiled. "Might be that you could," he said. "Later."

"I am off duty in thirty minutes," she whispered. "I know which cabin is yours. Would you like to . . . discuss your needs in private?" Her smile was marred slightly because her teeth were bad. Longarm figured he could forgive her that much.

"Half an hour then," he said, depositing his napkin beside his plate and standing. He hadn't realized just how small the girl was. He towered over her, and he guessed now that she would have to raise herself onto her toes in order to reach five feet.

49

Her eyes sparkled for a moment, then decorously dropped as she once more played out the role of waitress rather than coquette.

Cute, he thought as he headed out onto the deck for an after-dinner smoke. Call it a half hour's worth of relaxation out there, he thought. Then back to his cabin.

The girl was definitely cute.

Her name was Gia and she claimed to be twenty-six years old, although she certainly did not look it. Her skin had the taut, smooth elasticity of youth, and she was good to the taste.

Gia was so short he had to lift her up in order to kiss her. That did not seem an insurmountable problem.

She came into his cabin, winked at him, and delicately slid the bolt shut to lock the world away. She was a wanton little thing, and direct. There was no coy trifling or posturing about her. She locked the door and laughed and immediately stepped out of her dress, tossing it and her apron and the chemise she wore underneath all onto the bedside stand, where Longarm's gunbelt already lay.

Gia was one of those rare and wonderful girls who are at their loveliest when naked. She did not need any sort of artifice to improve upon what blunt nature gave her.

Her waist was tiny, her breasts high and firm with large, dark nipples. Her belly was flat above a patch of black, curling hair, and her thighs were slim and sleek.

Her teeth were not good, but her breath was sweet and clean. And her lips were delightfully soft.

Longarm cradled her in his strong arms and took his time about kissing her.

"You are beautiful," she whispered. "*Muy* handsome." She made a sound much like a kitten's purr and buried her face into the side of his neck. He could feel the tip of her tongue there as she licked and murmured.

He felt her tug at the side of his shirt and she whispered. "Please. It is in the way. I want to know the taste of your flesh, please."

Longarm kissed her some more, then set her down and let her help him swiftly out of his clothes.

Gia gasped when she saw the size of his cock. She gasped. And then she smiled. "So pretty, eh? So strong."

Gently, she reached out to touch him. She laughed when the very slight contract made his already erect and ready pecker jump and bounce.

She dropped to her knees and looked up at him past thick, curling eyelashes. Her eyes were huge and liquid. "Would you mind?"

"Go ahead," he told her.

Gia leaned forward, lips slightly parted. She held her face close to him and slowly breathed in, savoring the scent of his cock for a moment. Then steadying it with gentle fingertips. Touching it lightly with her tongue. First the shaft. Then, more firmly, his balls.

She licked his scrotum and very tenderly sucked first one nut and then the other into her mouth. She moaned a little.

She returned to his prick and ran her tongue up and down it. Pulled his foreskin back and lightly circled it with her tongue. Opened her pretty mouth wide and drew the head into the moist warmth of her mouth.

She sucked, long and slow, until Longarm felt his knees begin to grow weak. He touched the back of her head, then pulled back. He sat on the side of the bed. Hell, he needed to.

Gia smilingly followed, walking forward on her knees to the side of the bed.

She pressed her breasts against his erection, trapping his shaft in the valley between them. She looked into Longarm's eyes while she pressed her palms against the sides of her own tits so as to hold him more tightly between them.

After a moment, she rocked lightly back and forth on her knees, drawing him slowly in and out of the pocket of hot flesh she had created around him.

"Damn," he blurted out. "Careful there or I'll squirt all over you."

"Oh, no, please. Do not waste the juice of manhood. Never. It is mine. Let me have it, please."

She released her breasts and dipped her head to him again. Taking him into her mouth. Suckling. Slowly. In and out again. In. Deep. Sucking hard. Swirling her tongue around and around him while she held him inside her mouth.

It took only seconds more before Longarm felt the demanding rise of his explosion.

Took only moments before the sweet, driving flow of hot fluids burst out of him.

Gia gagged on the amount of come he spewed into her throat, but she overcame the impulse and stayed with him, continuing to suck and encourage the release of every last drop.

After a moment, she swallowed. Released his cock from the heat of her mouth and smiled up at him.

"It is good," she said. She sounded pleased with herself.

Hell, Longarm was mighty pleased with her too.

"I hope," he said, "you aren't in any hurry t' leave."

Her answer was to begin licking her way up his torso, lingering to lick and suckle each nipple as she went.

Longarm slipped his hand into the hot valley between her thighs. She was wet, the curly pubic hair already limp with the moisture of her juices.

This, he thought, was gonna be the most pleasant evening he'd spent in a long time.

Chapter 12

Gia gave pleasure with joyous abandon, and was equally passionate about receiving it. She gasped with delight when Longarm covered her tiny body and filled her with his huge shaft.

She wrapped herself tight around him, clinging fiercely with arms, legs, and mouth while urging him ever deeper into her flesh. Longarm had known many women who simply were not large enough to accommodate him, but despite her small size, Gia wanted everything he had and begged for more.

Her breathing was harsh and rasping from the extent of her efforts as her hips pumped and writhed beneath Longarm's thrusts, and she cried out in ecstasy within moments after he entered her.

"Don' stop. Please. Don' stop," she cried, her breath hot in his ear.

Longarm kissed her. And kept going.

Every dozen strokes or so, Gia would go into violent paroxysms of climactic pleasure. The girl was an explosion looking for an excuse to blow. Her frantic releases were so frequent and so vigorous that Longarm found himself wondering just how long she could keep this up.

He began to slow the pace of his own movements and to control the rise of his own pleasure, avoiding the outburst of semen that would put a halt to things, even if only a brief one. He was curious. Could Gia continue indefinitely?

After . . . he had no idea how many times she came. He hadn't known at the start that he would want to count. Eventually, she began to whimper when she climaxed, and it occurred to him that the repeated spasms, however pleasurable, had become genuinely painful for her. Yet even so, she clung to him, her body sleek with sweat, and pounded his belly with hers, grinding her plump little mound into him, slamming her body hard against his.

She was in pain but she would not stop.

Longarm let go then. Allowed himself the rise of his sap and the gush of his liquid essence deep into Gia's body.

His climax was all the more powerful for having been delayed, and this time he was the one who trembled and shuddered in powerful release.

Gia wept and quivered as she held him tight. She was slick with sweat and tears, and her breath was hot and salty when he kissed her.

Longarm raised himself from her, but she held him close and refused to let him go.

"Not yet. Stay. Inside me. So good. So good. Close your eyes. Stay. Thank you. Thank you. Thank you."

Longarm took most of his weight onto his knees and elbows, but continued to lie on top of the girl, who was thoroughly satiated . . . as he was himself now. He felt completely drained, his balls and belly emptied now and hollow.

"Sleep, dear one. Stay inside me, please. Close your eyes. Sleep," she encouraged, stroking his back lightly as she did so.

Longarm did not intend to sleep, but he did close his

eyes and allow himself to relax. He felt wrung out. Limp and loose and quite content.

He felt Gia's left hand leave his back while with the right she continued to stroke and soothe.

She extended her arm—he could feel the very slight shift of weight as the bed rocked just a little—and then there was a very faint, dull scrape of . . . he could not figure out what that very tiny sound was.

But it brought him to full alertness. He did not consciously know why such a tiny movement and indistinct sound should raise the hair on the back of his neck. But there was something . . . something . . .

Longarm flung his right arm out, striking Gia's forearm and pinning her hand to the damp and sweaty sheets.

She snarled and bucked beneath him, trying to throw his weight from her.

Trying with amazing strength to strike him with her left hand. With the . . . he could not even see what she held there. Something small. Something metal. Something sharp.

The weapon, whatever the hell it was, had been concealed within the clothing she'd so casually dropped onto the bedside stand before they made love.

Love. Jesus! No wonder her passions had been running so high. She was a black widow spider, eager to mate and then to kill.

Damn her!

Gia tried again to stab him, although he saw now that her method of assassination required a quiet, almost a cooperative victim, for it was no knife she held that could slash and cut, but only a somewhat shortened and very sharp ice pick, its handle reduced in size for concealment in the palm of Gia's small hand.

Damn her!

He grasped her wrist and squeezed. Hard. Bore down on flesh and bone as hard as he could. He heard a muffled

55

pop as something, bone or sinew or both, gave way.

Gia screamed.

The ice pick clattered onto the cabin floor beside the well-used bed, and Gia struggled violently to tear free from him.

She hissed curses in Spanish. Tried to bite him. Spat, her sputum landing on his shoulder and the side of his neck and sliding unpleasantly across his skin.

"Hold still, dammit," he grumbled.

Despite the injury to her wrist, she continued to jerk and pull in an effort to tear herself free, and she continued to berate him with dire threats and ugly imprecations in language that he fortunately did not understand.

"Hold still, will you? I don't want to hurt you any more'n I already have. Now just let me try an' reach my handcuffs over there. . . ."

Gia rolled her hips. Longarm knew what was coming next. He blocked her knee with his thigh to keep her from turning his balls into mush.

"Look, you might 's well relax. The game is up an' there's no damn way an eighty-pound midget like you is gonna overpower me. So calm down an' let me get those cuffs on you. I don't want t' hurt you, Gia. Now let me get up an' get those cuffs an' you and me can have us a nice, calm talk. That's all. Talk. *Comprende*?"

She said something in Spanish that he was pleased to not understand. Then "All right. Let me up."

She stopped struggling and lay quiet beneath him.

"That's better." He smiled. "Seems an awful shame, though, to ruin what up till you tried to kill me was looking t' be a mighty nice evening. Hell, I coulda gone again a couple times if you hadn't went an' spoiled it."

Her eyes went wide as he eased off the bed and took a step backward toward the chest where his manacles lay.

"I thought you were all used up," Gia said, startled.

"Not yet. Seems a pity, don't it."

She rolled her eyes. "I would have waited. You know?"

"Yeah, well, under the circumstances, I reckon it's just as well we stopped when we did. Any more and I might've been so tired I really would've dropped off to sleep, an' then where would we be?"

Gia did not answer that. But they both knew the answer.

"Stay still now. I'm not gonna hurt you." He fumbled on the top of the chest for the handcuffs. He did not feel them, and glanced in that direction.

In the instant when his attention was diverted trying to find the handcuffs, Gia launched herself off the bed, grabbing for Longarm's gunbelt and the .44 Colt it held.

"I told you, dammit. . . ."

He was quicker than she was, and the cabin was not so big that any one part of it was very far from any other.

Longarm stepped forward.

Gia's hand closed over the small end of Longarm's holster.

His hand closed over her already damaged wrist.

The girl screamed in pain. Dropped the gunbelt. It hit the floor with a dull, heavy thump.

"Will you please hold still, dammit?"

Gia snarled. Squirmed. But not in the throes of pleasure this time.

She tried to kick him. Tried to snatch her arm out of his grasp. Tried with her free hand to scratch his eyes out.

"I swear, girl, you ain't nothing but a damn little wildcat. Now settle down before I have to go an' hurt you again."

She bit him, clamping strong teeth onto his wrist.

"Damn you, girl, that hurts. Now leave be."

He tried to shake her off. Couldn't.

"Gia. Quit! D'you hear me? Quit it."

If anything, she was biting all the harder. It hurt like hell, and if she kept this up she was going to draw blood.

57

He'd heard it said that the bite of a human person is much more dangerous and likely to turn bad than the bite of a dog even.

"Dammit, Gia."

She clung to his wrist with her teeth and with her free hand, and she acted like she was not going to let go until she bit his hand clean off, damn her.

Longarm sighed.

But gentlemanly impulses only run so deep. His were pretty much used up as far as little Gia was concerned.

Longarm balled his left hand into a rock-hard fist and let fly with a sharp and very hard blow to the side of her jaw.

The punch was just about as hard as he could manage to throw, and it hit perfectly square.

Gia went loose and limp and her teeth lost their hold on him.

She fell over, falling on top of the gunbelt on the floor.

"Oh, no, you don't," he said. "We aren't having none of that."

He quickly stepped forward to grab his gunbelt and get it out of her reach, then felt around beneath her very limp body until he found the ice pick she'd dropped earlier. He retrieved it and put both the ice pick and the revolver well out of reach on top of the chest.

He picked up the handcuffs that were there and bent over Gia's motionless form.

He found her wrist, the undamaged one, and lifted it so he could snap the steel cuff onto it.

Then, frowning, he knelt and examined the girl more closely.

Once he'd done that, he sighed and tossed the handcuffs onto the bed. He would not be needing them.

Longarm did not know if his punch had done it, or if Gia had hit the side of the bed table when she went down.

But for whatever reason, and however it had happened, the small girl's neck was broken.

She was as dead as she'd wanted him to be.

Dammit. Dammit! What a horrid, horrible waste.

Longarm sat on the side of the bed. It still smelled of sweaty lovemaking.

He felt . . . weary. As if the weight of the world lay on his shoulders and was crushing him.

What a terrible, terrible waste this was.

Chapter 13

The captain did not look happy. He motioned for the first mate and two of the hands to join him, then led the way forward to the quiet at the bow of the long riverboat. "May I ask, sir, to see your credentials?"

Longarm understood. Hell, he'd come aboard as a complete stranger, announced himself as a peace officer . . . and then proceeded to kill two people, never mind that both were in self-defense or that Gia's death was an accident. He very carefully fished inside his coat for his wallet, flipped it open to display his badge, and handed it to the captain. The mate and pair of burly hands were watching very attentively. Obviously, they were present to lend assistance in case this crazed killer on board decided to leap at their captain.

The man took his time examining Longarm's badge, then closed the wallet and returned it. He told the deckhands they could leave, but prudently kept his first officer beside him.

"You say the girl's death was an accident?"

"Yes. She attacked me with a cut-down ice pick. Here." Longarm produced the deadly little weapon, its tip ground to a needle point, and gave it to the boat's captain. "Like

I already told you, I took that away from her, and she bit me. You can see the tooth marks here." He pushed his sleeves up to expose his wrist, where dark bruises and brighter red marks would likely remain for several days.

"I punched her and she fell. I don't know if it was me hitting her or her head striking the bed table that broke her neck. Not that it makes any difference, I suppose. She's dead. I wish she wasn't. I'd damn sure like to know why she tried to kill me."

"And what, may I ask, was the young lady doing in your cabin, Marshal?"

"Let's just say that she wasn't a lady," Longarm told him. "It's obvious from how she handled herself that she's done this sort of thing before. She had me . . . it'd be fair t' say that she had me mighty relaxed by the time she made her move. Slipped the ice pick out of the clothes she'd tossed on the table. Would've jammed it into the back of my skull or spine, I suppose, if I hadn't caught on in time. There's a little hollow, it's right back here." Longarm demonstrated, feeling of the soft spot low on the back of the skull.

"One jab in there and you're gone. Instant. I doubt there'd even be much pain from it. Prob'ly not a helluva lot of pain from a broken neck either, I'd think. Point is, Captain, the girl was a pro. And a member of your crew."

The captain—his name was Abraham Lytle—frowned. "I remember her. And unlike the fake waiter, Marshal, this girl was indeed one of our employees. She hired on in Omaha. At the last minute. I hadn't expected to need anyone, but one of our regular girls failed to report in time for sailing. I needed a replacement in a hurry."

"I hate t' say this, Captain, but I wouldn't be real surprised if that missing employee is dead too. Or somehow incapacitated deliberately so there'd be an opening for this assassin."

"She was a pretty little thing," the captain said. "I re-

61

member her very well. But she did not appear to be overly interested in male companionship. I happen to know that several of our other people"—he looked at the first mate, who blushed a little—"tried to become better acquainted with her during her short stay aboard. She rebuffed them, and in no uncertain terms. Isn't that right, Paul?"

"She had a sharp tongue on her," the first mate said. "I took a crack at her, I admit it. She acted like she was gonna snatch my head off and throw it to the fish."

"That was nothing personal, I'd say," Longarm told him. "Gia was a professional. She wouldn't have wanted any distraction with personal involvement. Wouldn't have wanted to risk some crew member becoming jealous and ruining things when she was trying to set up her target. It's no wonder she refused you."

"You really think she came aboard for the express purpose of murdering a United States marshal?"

Longarm didn't bother quibbling about the distinction between a marshal and a deputy. He merely said, "Yes, sir, I do believe that."

"Why?"

"Captain Lytle, that is exactly what I would've wanted to ask Gia. Why. And who hired her for the job."

In truth, Longarm was fairly sure he knew why, or at least the surface reason for the murder attempt. Longarm was there to "escort" and protect the Marquis de Sant Cerre. Someone wanted the marquis. But wanted him alive, wanted to kidnap him. Longarm's presence made that difficult. Therefore, the difficulty had to be removed so the primary task could be completed. Kill Longarm. Kidnap Jean-Claude Gilbert. Simple.

Whoever was behind this, and for whatever reason, they had sent at least a two-person team aboard at Omaha. A primary killer, the waiter, and a backup, Gia.

Longarm's question now was whether a third killer had been deemed necessary to back up the backup.

He doubted it.

But he did not intend to stake his life on that assumption. For the remainder of this job he was going to have to be damned vigilant.

"I'm sorry about all of this, Captain," Longarm said. "And, uh, I expect some of your people will take care of removing the body from my cabin?"

"I will see to it. Of course."

"You might let them know ahead of time that she's naked. It could come as something of a shock if they just walk in and find her on the floor like that."

"I'll take care of it myself," the first mate said.

Longarm suspected the man wanted a chance to see what Gia'd had underneath her clothes. But why not? Gia wouldn't care. Not now. Let the man have an eyeful if he liked. It would be something he could bring back to mind at night when he whacked off.

"Take a passkey with you," Longarm advised him. "I locked the door. Didn't think it would be a good idea for anybody to walk in an' find her."

"Yes, of course." Paul excused himself and headed for the ladder.

"I hope you didn't take on any other hands at the last moment in Omaha," Longarm said to Lytle.

"No, Marshal. She was the only one."

"All right, then, Captain. An' believe me, I'm sorry I've had to trouble you with this. I hope it won't happen again. Will you be putting in soon to dispose of the body? Or anything?"

"We'll take on wood later this afternoon. It's a regularly scheduled stop."

"Will there be a telegraph office at the landing? I need t' bring my boss up to date about all this."

"I'm sure there is, Marshal. We should be there about an hour. If that isn't long enough for you, I can hold the boat . . . under the circumstances."

63

"I doubt there will be any need for that, sir, but I thank you for the offer." Longarm touched the brim of his Stetson and excused himself.

He headed down to the salon—he couldn't go back to his cabin yet anyway, not until Gia's corpse was removed—for a whiskey and a cigar.

Damned riverboat trips were supposed to be relaxing, he mused on his way down. Funny, but he sure as hell wasn't feeling very relaxed.

Chapter 14

"Tell me something," Longarm said over a snifter of the best damn brandy he'd ever tasted. Not that he was an authority on brandies. On rye whiskey maybe. Or rotgut Injun whiskey. But not on brandy.

"Yes, of course."

"Why are we starting this search from New Orleans?"

Jean-Claude shrugged. "It is where the guard detail entered this country, no? It is where their journey began. Therefore it is where we shall start ours."

"My point is that somebody other than you an' me has an interest in this. That's obvious. An' whoever they are an' whatever they want in the long run, right now they want you. Wanted me outta the way so they can get to you. That much is plain."

"Yes? So?"

"So by now maybe they know the assassins failed ... like if they was supposed to send a telegraph confirming the kill ... but it just could be that this other party assumes I'm dead an' they can meet you at the boat in N'Orleans."

"That sounds correct, yes."

"So I been thinking maybe we shouldn't be on the boat when it hits the city."

"What choice do we have?"

"Hell, Jean-Claude, how many landings are there between here an' there. N'Orleans is still two days downriver. And it's only a starting point. There have t' be other places mentioned on whatever map or diary it is that you're pretending you don't have. . . ."

"M'sieur." Gilbert adopted a shocked and wounded look. "How can you say such a thing as this?"

Longarm managed to keep from laughing, but for a moment there it was touch and go. The marquis's shock was about as fake as Gia's passion had been. "Jean-Claude, what I was told is that a map and diary turned up not long ago. That's why you and me are here. The way I figure it, the original documents are very likely somewhere in France right now." Longarm smiled. "But you pretty much have t' have copies with you. How else could you expect to find the gold? You either have detailed copies on your possession, or you've memorized them to the point that you're acting as a copy yourself. Either way, that's why somebody would want to kidnap you. I'm saying they want the gold and they want you so's they can get it. Am I right?"

"It is your story. Please proceed."

"Jean-Claude, it has t' be right. You didn't start this deal without some sort of destination in mind. Either a destination or a route or key so you can find the right place. Prob'ly not an actual destination or you wouldn't need me, I'm thinking. You'd just go there and reclaim your things and be done with it. So what it comes down to, you have some way t' know where we're to look. My job is to keep you out o' the hands of those other folks while you're looking."

"Yes?"

"So what I'm saying, Jean-Claude, is that we oughta

let this boat go on to New Orleans without us. I think we oughta get off at Baton Rouge tomorrow."

Gilbert scowled. Then nodded. "*Oui*. This is sensible. But I 'ave already engaged freighters to meet us at the wharf. To bring my baggage, no?"

"Definitely no," Longarm told him. "Anybody hired ahead of time like that . . . we couldn't be certain the whole damn crowd of them wasn't part of the opposition, like that fake waiter and the girl and the kidnappers back in Omaha. No, we're way better off to leave at Baton Rouge unannounced. Let your downriver freighters show up lookin' for you. That oughta keep the other folks busy while we slip away with a good head start on them."

"If you say so. But it will be a nuisance."

"I dunno about you, Jean-Claude, but I'd a damn sight rather be annoyed than shot dead. Or in your case, kidnapped an' prob'ly tortured. Now pour me another belt of that anemic likker, will you? For grape juice it ain't entirely awful."

Baton Rouge was a typical river town. Ramshackle, sun-baked, and existing largely to handle the collection and shipment of cotton. In the South, cotton still was king.

One benefit to this was that there were dozens, perhaps hundreds of wagons available for hire. One wagon with a waterproofed tarpaulin stretched over the cargo box was enough to transport Jean-Claude's bags and boxes and crates and bundles. The Frenchman also hired a fully enclosed opera buggy for himself and Longarm to ride in.

They might very well end up dead, Longarm reflected, but they would damn sure ride to their deaths in great comfort.

The two drivers took care of transferring Gilbert's mountain of gear from the wharf onto the freight wagon, and they were ready to go.

"You wouldn't mind telling us where-at we're bound,

would you?" the owner of the buggy asked Longarm. "My wife will want to know where we're going and when she can expect me back."

"Friend," Longarm said, "if I knew I'd sure tell you, but all I'm doing is following him." He pointed toward Gilbert, who was rather fussily supervising the positioning of certain of his boxes. Apparently, he liked to have easy access to the essentials. Like his wines and brandies and cordials and liqueurs.

"I already asked him. He claimed he doesn't know."

"Then I sure don't either," Longarm said. "Sorry."

"The one that's gonna be sorry," the driver complained, "is me. My wife is gonna be royally pissed." He snorted. "I get fifteen feet from her skirt hem and she thinks it's another skirt I'm looking for."

"Does she have reason to be suspicious?" Longarm asked.

"Well, sure. But that doesn't mean I got to like her doing like that," the driver said, his voice and his expression indignant at the thought of such matrimonial mistrust.

Longarm laughed. "Come on. It looks like he's about done over there."

"Give me a second to write out a note and send it off to my missus telling her I might not be home for a couple months. Then I'll be set to go."

"Oh, I don't know that the job will take all that long," Longarm said. "It could just be for the next week or two."

The driver winked. "Yeah, but I might could be gone for a couple months anyhow, mister."

Longarm crawled into the comfortably appointed buggy and waited for Jean-Claude to join him so they could head out.

Chapter 15

Traveling with the marquis was . . . different.

Longarm could not claim that he enjoyed it worth a damn, but he had to concede that it was a comfortable way to go.

Longarm laid out his bedding under the opera coach, and the hired hands slept beneath the freight wagon. The marquis, however, was not willing to rough it like some lowly commoner.

At night, a tent had to be erected for Gilbert's comfort and privacy, complete with a thick rug for a floor, a folding cot, a folding table, and folding chairs. Supper and breakfast were taken on china, which of course had to be washed, dried, and packed away again before their tiny two-vehicle train could get under way again. It was no damned wonder the man dragged so much baggage along with him.

It was also no damned wonder they moved at a pace considerably slower than that set by handcart immigrants who walked the whole way westward.

"Y'know, Jean-Claude, give it a couple more days and whoever is after you is gonna catch up again."

"But, m'sieur. We have . . . the phrase, I believe, is 'given them the slip,' no?"

"Dammit, Jean-Claude, that was only three days ago. If they're really pushing it, they could be on our tail again before nightfall."

"But they do not know where we are going," the Frenchman insisted. "How can they find us?"

"Hell's clangin' bells, Jean-Claude, there's a thousand roads a fella could take from Baton Rouge. The problem is that there's only one good one if you're heading west. That's this highway right here. Whoever is after you isn't likely t' be as flat-ass dumb as you are when it comes to this here country. They're bound to know. Or anyways be bright enough to ask somebody. An' if you're heading west, which we seem to be, this here is the road we have to take. This or else detour all over the damn countryside."

"It is uncivilized to travel like an animal." He shuddered. "To sleep on the ground . . . *non*. Never. What was that you said about my intelligence?"

"I didn't say shit about your intelligence," Longarm grumbled.

"We will go now." Gilbert's expression clearly stated that this was a closed subject as far as he was concerned. He left the table—left it for the two drivers to pack up and put away—and sat haughtily on the rich leather of the carriage seat.

Longarm held his tongue—it wasn't easy—and walked a few paces away so he could light a cheroot and get control of his temper.

Ordinarily, he would have been glad to bear a hand with the daily chores rather than throw everything onto the backs of the drivers, but not this trip. That would only put him into the same category as any other hired hand in Jean-Claude Gilbert's view. Which he was to some extent already. Longarm did not want to let that situation get any worse than it already was.

70

He did, however, have a word in private with the two drivers so they would perhaps be able to understand.

Nevertheless, he did feel bad about standing idle while they performed the labor inherent in the camp chores.

"So where exactly is it that we're going?" Longarm asked at lunch. At least, thank goodness, Gilbert did not insist on having his tent set up and a full meal prepared for their midday meal. He did want the table and chairs brought out, but those unfolded quickly and were actually a pretty pleasant change from having to sit cross-legged on the ground or find a stump to perch on.

"West. Further to the west, I think," the marquis said, picking suspiciously at the edges of a slice of cold ham.

"You think? D'you mean you don't *know*?" Longarm asked with no small measure of surprise.

"Soon I shall have to rely upon your knowledge of this country, I think," Gilbert admitted.

"I don't understand."

"There are things referenced ... not place names ... that a visitor would not know. It was hoped a man such as yourself would know these things."

"I think it's about time you showed me what it is that we're gonna take our directions from," Longarm told him.

"But of course." Gilbert reached inside his coat and drew out a trifold wallet of elegantly tooled kidskin. "Here. And here."

The first document was a sketch. Longarm would not go so far as to claim it was a map. Rather a very crude sort of sketch. It showed a lump—which, depending on scale, could either have been a boulder or an entire mountain—and a squiggle that might be a river or stream. And three upright marks with little branches jutting out from the tops. Trees, obviously. Or possibly a whole damn forest.

"Where's this supposed to be?" Longarm asked.

"I do not yet know," Gilbert admitted. "That we must learn from this." He handed over the second piece of paper, this one covered in writing.

"I can't read this. It's in French."

Gilbert shrugged. "I can. You will understand that these are copied from the originals. Those were yellowed and difficult to read. I have myself seen them, however. These copies are faithful to the originals. They tell us everything the unknown writer of them left for us to follow.

"Unfortunately, they were not intended to be directions for others to comprehend. They were means by which he himself could find his way back to the gold. So he could reclaim it for himself, one must assume."

"Why'd he leave the gold behind in the first place?" Longarm asked.

"This we may never know. The orders of superior officers perhaps. An attack by your wild Indians. This he does not say. I too would like to know."

Indians. That implied somewhere on or beyond the frontier, at least as it had existed during those years. "And this tells us that we're going . . . ?"

"West." Jean-Claude stretched and peered at the sky, where distant clouds threatened rain later in the afternoon. "One more glass of the wine, I think. Then we shall go."

"Sure. Whatever you say." Longarm rolled his eyes. But he turned his head away first so the Frenchman would not see.

72

Chapter 16

"But m'sieur, it is not possible to travel in this weather. It would be totally beyond civility, no?"

"No, dammit," Longarm insisted. "Look, Jean-Claude, we need t' get off this main highway and find our way along the back roads. We need to—"

"We need to stop here," the Frenchman said as he peered down his nose. His tone of voice left no room for argument. "We stop. Now."

Longarm had to admit that the place where Gilbert wanted to wait out the rain was probably the only hotel within forty miles.

Gilbert left instructions for the disposition of his baggage without bothering to first go inside and register, then strode imperiously indoors and demanded a suite and that a tub and hot water be brought to it immediately.

"You will also provide accommodation for my bodyguard and drivers. You may show me now to my rooms, m'sieur."

The poor fellow standing behind the desk looked thoroughly befuddled by Gilbert's whirlwind arrival.

"Why are you standing there gaping, eh? Move, man. Quickly, quickly."

The man moved. Quickly.

Longarm could only shake his head and go look for a drink, leaving the unloading and care of the animals to Max Dain and Carl Bonner, the drivers. Longarm felt sorry for the two of them for they suffered the bulk of the marquis's haughty disdain. On his way past, he told them, "I'm goin' up the street to the first saloon I see, an' I expect to be there for a spell. Come by when you're done here an' I'll buy you a drink or two."

"Damn, Longarm, I wish it was you we was working for instead of that frog-eater."

Longarm winked at them, and left them to their work while he hurried along to the saloon, his shoulders hunched and hat pulled low over his eyes. The cold, driving rain just kept coming.

The first saloon he came to was a small and quiet spot with an ornately carved and mirrored backbar, obviously not the sort of place where rowdiness and fighting were welcomed. The floors were swept clean rather than layered with sawdust, and the spittoons were polished to a bright, brassy gleam. There were no gaming tables, no whores, and no piano. And the bartender's shirt and apron were both immaculately clean.

"You wouldn't have a good rye whiskey here, would you, and maybe a decent smoke to go with it?"

"I can offer you the best of either," the barman said. He brought a redwood box out from beneath the bar surface and opened it to a display of several choices of cigar. Longarm selected one while the barkeep poured a glass of whiskey for him. Longarm nipped the twist off the end of the cigar, then swished that end around in the rye for a moment before lighting the dry end from a candle offered by the bartender. He took a deep puff on the cigar and a taste of the whiskey.

"Nice," he said.

"Which?"

"Both," Longarm assured him. He smiled. "Feels kind of like I've come home to Mother." The bartender looked pleased.

Longarm carried his whiskey to a vacant table near the door and examined the other patrons. They looked like town dwellers, for the most part wearing shoes instead of boots. Their clothing bore no road dust, and they looked like they were accustomed to regular visits to a barber. Longarm idly wondered what it must feel like to live in a small town, go to the same safe and unexciting job every day, see the same faces day after day. Must be peaceful, he thought.

But dull.

There might come a day, he supposed, when he would want something like this for himself.

But not today. Not today, thank you.

He tossed back the rest of the excellent rye and waited for Dain and Bonner to catch up with him.

"I'm horny, dammit. And I'm bored," Max Dain grumbled. "Where's the damn women? I never saw a place like this without women."

Max, Longarm had long since concluded, was not a gentleman to the manor born. Never saw a quiet saloon that prohibited the presence of ladies? That was almost as bad as never having seen the other kind. "Sit still," Longarm told him.

He went to the bar and spoke to the bartender. When he returned to the table, he told his companions, "There's a place about three blocks over. Looks like a house. It isn't."

"That sounds better," Dain said.

It was still raining hard enough to drown the fires of Hell, and the streets were a quagmire of brown, soupy mud, but there was sidewalk most of the way, and wide boards had been laid across the mud at the street intersections. That was one nice thing. There was no scarcity of pine timber in east Texas.

Longarm led the way to a tall, narrow structure that looked like it had been painted white at one time. Say, twenty or thirty years ago. There was not much paint remaining. A small porch stretched across the front, but there were no rocking chairs on it, nor was there a swing or a glider where someone could sit to enjoy a quiet evening. But then the residents here would not want to be seen any more than their visitors would.

It was not yet night, but lamplight beckoned warm and welcoming from behind closed draperies. Longarm and the two drivers dashed up the flagstone walk onto the porch, and Bonner gave the bellpull a tug.

The door was opened by a plump, matronly looking woman with fluffy white hair and naturally rosy cheeks. She would have seemed quite at home carrying a tray of freshly baked cookies and with her skirts surrounded by smiling grandchildren.

"Want to get laid, do you? Come in, boys, come in." Her voice sounded like she gargled twice daily with whiskey and gravel. So much for the grandmotherly look, Longarm thought.

Dain and Bonner marched happily inside. Longarm paused long enough to remove his Stetson and to brush as much water off himself as he could before he entered.

What the hell. It wasn't like he had any better plans for the evening.

Chapter 17

The cigars were good, the music wasn't awful, and the whiskey . . . two out of three isn't bad. But after the first shot he sent out for a pail of beer instead.

Actually, the place was kinda relaxed and friendly and pleasant. The girls were a happy lot if not very good-looking, and Longarm was enjoying himself.

"Are you sure you don't wanta go upstairs, honey?" a skinny blond girl with rabbit teeth and pimples asked for probably the tenth time.

"Not tonight, pretty girl. I'm too tired," he lied. "But tomorrow if I'm rested up, I'd sure like to."

"You'll pick me if you do?" she persisted.

"That's a promise, sweet thing."

She grinned and went off toward the kitchen, apparently satisfied that she still had what it took to drive the boys wild.

And so she did, Longarm noticed. Judging from the way Max Dain was eyeing her as she left the room, she would be the next girl he took upstairs. It was a trip Max had made twice already, each previous time with a different girl. No wonder Max liked to have some time away from his wife back home in Louisiana. She probably limited him to no more than four or five times a night.

Carl Bonner came down from his one and only but much longer excursion onto the second floor. He had chosen a dark-eyed Mexican girl who might have been attractive if she lost thirty or forty pounds.

Max asked Carl something and Carl nodded, then squeezed the girl's left cheek—the lower left cheek—making her jump a little. But she didn't lose her smile.

"Hey, Longarm," Max called across the by now fairly crowded room. "Carl says the señorita here is pretty good. You want her?"

Longarm smiled and shook his head. "No, thanks, Max. You go ahead."

"In that case, Longarm, reckon I will."

Carl passed temporary ownership of the plump girl over to Max, and the two headed for the staircase. They were almost bowled over by a hatchet-faced fellow in a swallowtail coat who hurried down the last few steps and bolted for the front door like he was fixing to throw up and wanted out into the bushes before he let fly.

The grandmotherly madam sidled over and pulled a straight-back chair close to the armchair where Longarm was relaxing. She sat down and leaned near. "Did I hear your friend right?"

"I expect that depends on what you heard, doesn't it," he said agreeably.

"I thought he called you Longarm."

"So he did."

"You wouldn't be. . . ."

"My friends call me that. My name is Custis Long."

"And would you happen to be a United States marshal?"

"Just a deputy, not a marshal," Longarm clarified.

"Bejaysus," the madam exclaimed. "Imagine. A famous man like you. And under my own roof."

"Famous?" he asked.

"Plenty famous in some quarters," she said. "Infamous in some others. And the devil himself to hear some tell it."

"I'll leave it for you to decide how you want to think of me then," Longarm said.

"Can I get you another drink?"

"I still have some of my beer."

"Oh, honey, I don't mean that horse piss I pour for my regular trade. I have some good stuff too."

"A little rye would be nice then. Just to take the chill out of the air, you understand."

The madam motioned for the scrawny blonde, who was just returning from the kitchen. "Kitten, this gentleman is Deputy U.S. Marshal Custis Long, the one they call Longarm. I know you've heard of him."

"Yes, ma'am." It was plain she'd never heard the name before in her life, but she was too polite to say so. Or did not want to contradict the boss. Whichever.

The madam fished a key out from between her breasts, slipped the cord that held it from around her neck, and handed the key to Kitten. "You know the liquor cabinet in my office, dearie."

"Yes, ma'am."

"I want you should fetch me the bottle of rye whiskey that's in there. And two of my nice crystal glasses. Hurry now, child."

Kitten hadn't been a child for a good fifteen or twenty years, but she hurried as she'd been bidden. She was back in short order with the bottle and glasses on a glossily japanned tray.

The old madam was correct. This whiskey indeed was better. In fact, it was excellent.

"Nice," he said.

"Have some more. On the house. So is everything you want here. You want one of my girls? Two or three of them at once? Just tell me how I can please," she said.

"Oh, I couldn't. . . ."

"No, really. Once word gets around that I've entertained Marshal Longarm himself, I'll have more gentlemen in here than I know what to do with." She laughed. "But I will think of something, trust me."

"I'm sure you will."

"Hmm. I wonder if Edna would rent me a few of her girls for a few days. Through the weekend, say. But . . . sorry . . . I'm probably boring you. Here. Have some more." He'd barely lowered the level in his glass, but she insisted on refilling it anyway. "How about a snack? Have you eaten?"

"Come to think of it, I reckon we haven't."

"Kitten? Come here, baby. Run wake Cleofa. Tell her to get a meal together for our distinguished guest. What would you like, sweetie? Steak? Pork chops? Anything you want."

"A steak would go nice now. And maybe some eggs. Soda biscuits. Milk gravy. Coffee perhaps."

"You heard the man, Kitten. Tell Cleofa."

"Yes, ma'am, right away."

Longarm had another swallow of the excellent rye and took a moment to enjoy being pampered. Maybe he wasn't some rich French high mucky-muck, but this was more than good enough for him.

Chapter 18

"You boys come back now, hear? You know you're always welcome here."

"Thank you, Mama Jones," Longarm said. Carl Bonner told her good night. Max went so far as to kiss her cheek and give the old madam a bawdy wink, which prompted her to laugh and squeeze his crotch. But then Max had given her a week's worth of business in this one evening.

The three of them headed back out into the street. The rain had subsided. The ground was still muddy, but should dry fairly quickly. Longarm thought they would be able to travel again come morning.

"Are you sure you don't wanta join us?" Carl asked him.

"No, thanks. I've had enough for one night," Longarm said. "My belly is full and I've got a nice whiskey warmth. I expect I'll go back to the hotel and turn in."

"Hell, Longarm, I'll even pay for a round if you come have one more with us," Dain said.

Longarm chuckled. "Are you sure you can afford it after all those trips upstairs with the ladies?"

"Aw, they gave me a discount price for being such a good customer," Max said. Longarm could not tell if he was joking or not actually. Lord knows, he deserved a cut rate considering the sheer volume of his business.

"Enjoy yourselves," Longarm said. He left the two drivers in front of Mama Jones's place, debating where they should go next to complete their evening of partying.

At the moment Longarm was more interested in getting some sleep than another drink. He yawned and started back toward the main street.

There was a bright yellow flash to his left and half a second later, the quick, zipping bee-drone of a bullet speeding past.

Longarm hit the ground—hit the mud, actually; damn stuff was cold and clammy and felt like shit—with his Colt in hand.

He'd spotted the muzzle flash out of the corner of his eye, and was not positive now just exactly where the shooter was hiding.

Probably in the deep shadows over . . . he aimed, waited.

Exactly. There was a second flash and the dull report of a large-caliber pistol.

This time Longarm was ready. He triggered an answering shot, then bounded to his feet and dashed forward and to his right, slipping and sliding in the mud, but gaining a better angle to fire into the alley where the shooter had made his stand.

A third shot spat from the darkness, and somewhere behind him he heard the clatter of breaking glass.

Longarm fired again, and this time he thought he heard a grunt in response. He definitely heard the sound of something falling. The grunt had been . . . what? Pain? Surprise? It could have been either, and he did not intend to take any chances on the basis of a half-heard noise in the night. The shooter could well be dead now, but Longarm was not about to stake his life on that assumption.

He wasn't dead, damn him. There was a fourth flash

and bang, and immediately thereafter the sound of running footsteps.

Longarm fired blindly down the alley and set out in pursuit.

The shooter should have one, maybe two cartridges remaining in his gun, and Longarm damn sure did not intend to give him time to reload.

He saw a flicker of movement at the far end of the alley. Saw a dark figure break out onto the street and dart to his left.

Longarm instantly altered his direction, running to his left also, to the end of the block and then down the street there. In all likelihood, the shooter was expecting him to chase him through the alley, and would now be at the far end waiting for Longarm to charge into view.

The problem with breaking off the direct pursuit, of course, was that now the fellow had time enough to set up another ambush. And to reload.

Longarm slowed. Stopped there on the street for a moment while he too reloaded, replacing the two spent cartridges and adding a sixth to the cylinder. For ordinary carrying purposes, it was sensible to leave one chamber empty so the hammer could rest on that one with no danger of an accidental discharge. Safety was not an issue right now. Firepower might be.

Longarm held the .44 ready and walked as lightly and silently as he could down the street toward the end of the block. The shooter should be somewhere down there. By now he should be getting nervous, though. Wondering why Longarm hadn't burst out of the alley mouth. By now he might well be moving again. He . . .

There!

Someone was moving. Crouched over. Backing up and keeping his attention to his right, toward the alley mouth where he seemed still to expect Longarm to be.

It had to be the shooter.

No, dammit, it *almost* had to be the shooter.

But it could conceivably be some innocent townsperson wanting to get the hell out of the way of all this gunfire.

Already, there were lights beginning to show at windows that had been dark when Longarm came out of the whorehouse.

And back at Mama Jones's everything had gone dark. Windows that showed warm lamplight a few minutes ago were blank and lifeless now. It seemed the old woman knew better than to draw attention to herself when there was shooting going on.

Somewhere a block or so down, a man's voice called out demanding to know what the noise was about, and dogs were barking all over town.

At the end of the block, the person Longarm could see stood upright. He was holding . . . Longarm couldn't be sure. It looked like he had a gun in his hand. It could as easily be a lunch pail. The man could be some innocent bystander caught in a crossfire while he was trying to go home from work.

Longarm had a clear shot. He could not take it. He did not want to risk shooting an innocent. Dammit.

"Halt! Put your hands up!" he called loudly.

The half-seen figure at the end of the block turned to face him.

Whatever he held in his hand was pointing in Longarm's direction.

But he still could not see. Could not fire. Could not be sure.

"Drop it!" he shouted. "Right now." He moved closer. Closer.

Once more there was a golden fireball and the booming crack of a gunshot as the shooter tried to kill him.

Chapter 19

Longarm heard the slug plop into the mud with a loud, wet slap, the sound coming from somewhere behind him. And the man did not have time enough to shoot another round.

The big Colt bucked in Longarm's hand, and his own sheet of fire gave brief light to the dark street.

The bullet took the gunman somewhere low in the stomach, doubling him over as if he had the world's worst bellyache. Longarm took aim and fired again, and because of the man's posture the heavy .44 slug impacted on the crown of the man's head. He dropped facedown into a mud puddle, so quickly dead he did not so much as make bubbles in the rainwater.

Longarm reloaded before he walked forward. That one was dead, but if you find a rat in the corn crib, you shouldn't assume it is the only one there.

Lights were shining through windows all around by now, but only after several minutes of silence had passed did anyone brave the street to gawk and marvel.

"Is there a town marshal?" Longarm asked the man standing nearest to him.

"Y-yes, sir."

Longarm couldn't tell if the man stuttered or if he was just that frightened. "Go get him."

"It's all right, Chester. I'm here." A tall man carrying a lantern stepped out of the crowd. "I'm Marshal Tompkin."

Longarm pulled out his wallet and opened it to show his badge as he introduced himself.

"I'd heard you were in town," Tompkin said. "I wanted to meet you but not under these circumstances." The local lawman raised his voice and said, "It's all right, folks. This man is an officer of the law." He directed the light from his lantern onto the dead man lying at their feet. "What was this all about?" he asked.

"Damn if I know," Longarm admitted. "I came outside and started back to the hotel. Next thing I know this asshole is shooting at me. Let's turn him over. If I can see who he is, maybe I'll have some idea why he shot at me."

Tompkin rolled the body onto its back. The face was badly distorted by the shock of Longarm's bullet pushing outward from inside the skull cavity, and to make matters worse it was caked with mud.

"Shit, I couldn't recognize my own brother like this," Tompkin said. "Lou, fetch me a pail of water, will you? Use the fire bucket beside Leon's rain barrel in the alley there."

"Right away."

Tompkin dashed the bucket of water onto the dead man's face. That helped, although the distortion remained.

"I've seen him," Longarm said, "but I've no idea who he was except up until a couple hours ago he was a customer in Mama Jones's place. I noticed him because he was in such a hurry to leave he almost ran over a friend of mine getting out of there."

"Somebody on the run who thought you were after him?" Tompkin suggested.

Longarm shrugged. "Could be." And it could. But then

it could also be that the hatchet-faced fellow was one of the ones who were sure to be out looking for the Marquis de Sant Cerre. It seemed a shame they couldn't ask him. Longarm did not mention any of that to the local man, though. "Is he local?"

Tompkin looked the dead man over carefully, then shook his head. "It's hard to say for sure seeing as how he's all puffed out like that. But I don't believe I've ever seen him before. You say he was over at Mama's?"

"That's right."

"We'll ask her. If there's anybody in town who knows everybody in town, it would be Mama." Tompkin smiled. "The menfolk anyway. I wouldn't say she's all that well acquainted with the ladies."

"No, I'd think not. It's a good idea, though. Let me check his pockets first just in case that tells us anything."

A few minutes later, the marshal asked, "Well?"

Longarm shook his head. "A pocketknife. Half a box of .44 cartridges. Thirty-seven dollars in coin." Longarm handed the money to Tompkin. "That ought to be enough to pay for his burying anyway."

Tompkin detailed four men to carry the body off to the care of someone named James, presumably the undertaker or perhaps the coroner. Or both. "Let's see what Mama has to say," he said to Longarm.

The crowd was already dwindling, all the excitement over with and now not even a body to stare at. Longarm sometimes wondered what the fascination was all about. But it seemed the more staid and sheeplike the citizen, the more likely he was to gape and stare at someone else's violent ending.

The two lawmen were met at the door by the white-haired Mama Jones.

"You heard what happened, Mama?"

"Of course. Come in." She made a face. "Longarm,

dearie, you look perfectly awful. You're all covered with mud."

"I could've stayed on my feet and got shot instead," Longarm told her.

"Well, in that case . . ."

She ushered them inside. Longarm noticed that the presence of the town marshal had no effect on the other customers. Mama Jones, however, quickly shooed them out. "Sorry, boys. We're closed for the rest of the night. But y'all come back tomorrow. I know who you are. Tomorrow night you'll get a discount for your trouble. Half price on all service."

On that note the gents, there were five of them, were smiling when they left despite having their evening cut short.

Before she returned her attention to Tompkin, Mama Jones issued instructions that the girls should tell Cleofa to heat extra water. They were to bring the tub into the parlor here, then everyone was to gather. Everyone.

"Missy's sick, ma'am."

"She's not sick, she's lazy. And I said everyone."

"Yes, ma'am."

The girls fluttered away on their mission, and Mama Jones asked Tompkin to explain, which he quickly did.

"Pinched-in face and a swallowtail coat? Sure, I remember him. Nobody I've seen before, though. He didn't say much. Never gave a name that I know of. Wait a minute." She raised her voice. "Nelda!"

There was a clatter of footsteps and a smiling, moon-faced little redhead came running. "Yes, ma'am?"

Mama Jones described the man and added, "I believe he spoke with you earlier. I want you to tell the marshal here everything he said."

The girl frowned in thought for a moment, then said, "He didn't say all that much really. Just wanted to have me. Get it off and get it over with. He didn't want nothing special. Didn't even feel me up much. He never gave me a name, so I just called him 'Honey.' He picked me and paid me, climbed on top and rooted around for a couple minutes, then he got off, pulled his pants up, and left. Never took his clothes off and never said good-bye neither. I didn't like him. But he paid two dollars, so he was entitled to do it however he wanted."

"That's all? He said nothing personal? Not where he was from, nothing?"

"No, ma'am."

"Not even downstairs?"

"No, ma'am. He didn't make any small talk. Just pointed to me and then pointed upstairs. I nodded yes, and we went up. I was still up there cleaning myself when he left. I couldn't tell you anything after that."

"My girls all wash themselves," Mama Jones said proudly. "Wash inside and out, every customer, no matter what they want or where."

"Thank you, Nelda," Longarm said.

"Yes, sir. Is that all, ma'am?"

"Yes. Go help the others with that tub now, please." Mama Jones turned back to the men. "Sorry," she said. "I know that isn't much help."

"You tried." Longarm turned toward the door.

"And where do you think you are going now, Longarm?" Mama Jones asked.

"Back to the hotel. This cold mud feels awful. It's got my clothes sticking to my skin like cold cow crap."

"Why do you think I'm having the tub filled? Hmm? Gerald, if you don't have any more business here, you can leave now. My girls are going to take care of Marshal Long."

Tompkin chuckled. "Whatever you say, Mama."

"I do say. Now you may leave us alone, if you please."

Tompkin touched the brim of his hat and, with a grin directed toward Longarm, left the whorehouse.

By then the girls—there turned out to be eight of them—were grunting and huffing, dragging a huge copper tub into the middle of the parlor floor.

The cook, whose abilities in the kitchen Longarm had already sampled earlier, came in bearing the first of what would have to be many buckets of steaming hot water to begin the process of filling the big tub. Which, Longarm noticed, was big enough to hold two people. Or perhaps three nicely friendly ones.

"What about my clothes?" Longarm asked.

"Just get yourself out of them, dearie," Mama Jones said. "We have a fellow in town who does cleaning. Lord knows he owes me enough favors. I'll have him work on your things overnight. By the time you walk out of here tomorrow morning, they will be clean and dry, and you'll never know they were so bedraggled and filthy now."

While she was saying that, the ladies of the house were pouring hot water into the tub, then peeling themselves out of their own clothing.

Longarm found himself surrounded by naked women, each smiling and intent on taking care of his needs. All of them.

"Well, then," he said, clearing his throat. "A boy'd have to be a complete idiot to pass up an offer like this, wouldn't he."

Longarm did not consider himself to be an idiot, nor did he intend to act like one.

Chapter 20

By the time Longarm walked—he would have crawled except it would've been so undignified—out from among all those party-happy girls, he was drained. Empty. Hollow. His knees were weak and his head light, and it was just a damn good thing he did not have to ride a horse today or he surely would've fallen off. Fortunately, you can't very well fall out of an opera coach.

If, that is, they traveled. The rain had slacked off to something halfway between a drizzle and a heavy mist, but the roads were still apt to be muddy and near impassable.

For once, though, Longarm would welcome a chance to lay about, just stay in the hotel and recuperate.

It is not easy, he'd learned, to take on eight eager women all at the same time.

He'd managed it. But it hadn't been easy.

Still, thoughts of the previous night had to bring a smile to his face. Once he'd given in to the inevitable . . . it was a night to remember.

He made his way back to the hotel on legs that felt no more sturdy than wet rawhide. It was a wonder he didn't collapse facedown in the mud and soil his clothes all over again. And he certainly did not want to do that after Mama Jones had them cleaned so nicely for him.

The morning was well advanced by the time Longarm got there. He found Jean-Claude Gilbert already downstairs at breakfast. Longarm pulled out a chair and joined him, but refused a waiter's offer of breakfast. Longarm had already gorged himself on a magnificent breakfast over at Mama Jones's house. "Just coffee, thanks."

"Yes, sir." The waiter bowed and departed, then returned moments later with Longarm's coffee.

"I s'pose you'll be wanting to hole up here for another day," Longarm told the Frenchman. "The roads are still bad."

"Non," Gilbert said curtly. "We go. Immediate."

Longarm raised an eyebrow.

"This town. Pfft! Very bad place."

"You heard about the shooting?" Longarm asked.

"Shooting? Who cares about shooting. Let them all shoot each other. Let the survivors shoot themselves. We leave from here immediate."

"What's got your hackles raised this morning, Jean-Claude?"

"This place, it is not civilized. Do you know I 'ad to spend the night by myself? Alone? Ffft! I ask for a woman to be brought. The imbecile doorman goes, comes back, tells me all are taken. None are left for me. Me! Do you hear? None?" Jean-Claude looked grievously offended by that thought.

Longarm quickly lifted his coffee cup to his mouth, even though it was still much too hot to drink. He needed to hide the smile he could not keep from pulling at his lips. He suspected it was a very good thing that Jean-Claude Gilbert did not know exactly why he'd had to spend an entire night by himself. Alone. As he so sadly put it.

"Where 'ave you been, eh? Never mind. I told the man

to load your things into the coach. It and the wagon should be outside by now. We go as soon as I finish this poor excuse for a meal." He rolled his eyes. "The bread. Do you see this?" He waved a biscuit under Longarm's nose. "This . . . thing . . . this is not bread. This is dough that has been made hard. But bread?" He rolled his eyes again.

Gilbert finished eating and abruptly left the table, leaving Longarm sitting there with half a cup of coffee still before him. "We go. Now," the marquis snapped, even more rude and imperious than usual.

Longarm grumbled a little to himself. But he left the coffee behind and wobbled shakily out front. The coach and the wagon indeed were out there waiting, Jean-Claude already inside the coach.

It took real effort for Longarm to force his legs up the step and into the coach. He hadn't gotten a moment of sleep during the night. Not that he had any regrets. But it would be nice to make up for that now.

He tucked himself into a corner of the back-facing seat in the small coach, and was asleep before Max snapped the team into motion.

Longarm woke up thinking about that shooter the night before. Never mind that the nameless sonuvabitch was dead. The point was that he'd made the try. And Longarm had no idea why. Was he a fugitive with a guilty conscience who heard the name and jumped to the conclusion that Longarm had to be there chasing his sorry ass? Or was he working for whatever group it was who wanted Jean-Claude?

Longarm would not be particularly concerned if the man was just another felon on the run. If that were the case, that was the end of it.

But if the would-be kidnappers were closing in, that was indeed cause for alarm.

"Where are we?" he asked. He removed his Stetson and ran a hand over his head to smooth down his hair, and across his face to judge the state of his whiskers—he needed a shave as well as that haircut he'd never gotten around to—then knuckled the sleep out of his eyes. The process was not as good as a splash of cold water, but it did help a little.

"Texas," Jean-Claude said. He sounded irritable.

"You still mad because you didn't have a woman last night?"

"I am not mad. I am angry. Not because of the women in that stupid town, no. Because I am tired of this rain. Rain, rain, more rain. Mud, filth, nuisance. And Texas. How much longer before we get to New Mexico, eh?"

"I didn't know we was going to New Mexico."

"Well, we are. I think." He shrugged. "Maybe so."

"You think. You don't know," Longarm said.

Gilbert hesitated, as if reluctant to part with any information that he did not absolutely have to give away. "There is a place called Gros Teton, yes?" He did not pronounce it the way an American would have, but Longarm had no trouble understanding what he meant.

"There is such a place, sure."

"In Texas."

"That's right."

"Also in New Mexico."

"Right again," Longarm agreed.

"We are going to Gros Teton," Gilbert said.

"Which one?"

The Frenchman sighed. "This I do not know. Both of them if we must."

"Like if we don't find what you're looking for in the first one, we'll go on to the next, is that it?"

"Exactly so, yes."

"D'you know there's a Gros Teton in southern Colorado too? It's in the San Luis Valley not far north o' the New Mexico border."

Jean-Claude did not look at all happy to receive that bit of news. Not that Longarm was so damn thrilled about it himself. If the south of Colorado or New Mexico or anyplace in the west of Texas was where they were bound, it would've been a helluva lot easier to get there by heading south from Denver instead of going to all the bother of making the riverboat trek down to New Orleans—well, all right, Baton Rouge as it turned out.

He frowned. Or did Gilbert have some reason to do it that way? Some reason, that is, apart from a lack of knowledge about the geography of this country.

Longarm peered out into the gray, dreary day. A fine drizzle continued to fall, and the horses were making hard work of it.

"That you, Longarm?"

"It's me, Max."

"We're gonna have to make a long stop at the next place we come to. These horses is getting awful tired."

"Whatever you think best."

"Make it a place where good food is to be found," Gilbert put in.

Max did not bother to answer, but Longarm knew good and well that the man would stop where he thought the horses would best be tended and never mind the arrogant Frenchman.

Longarm settled back onto his seat and tugged the brim of his Stetson low, feigning sleep so he would not have to put up with Gilbert's conversation while they traveled.

Chapter 21

There was no town, just a crossroads with a store on one corner, a ramshackle house on another, and two small fenced enclosures holding goats on one side of the road and a mule on the other.

"What d'you think, Max?" Longarm asked when they came to a halt outside the store.

"I think we'd best lay over here for a few hours. There's hay in that shed over yonder. I'd like to buy some. Maybe even take our animals out of harness and turn them into the trap there to rest a bit." He squinted up at the sky, which had become lighter. The drizzle was nearly ended, and it looked like the rain would cease altogether very soon.

"I agree," Carl Bonner said, coming up from his wagon to join them. "My team is about worn down from all this sticky mud. We'll let them rest a bit an' the road dry while they're doing it."

"Why are we stopping here?" Jean-Claude grumbled as he climbed out of Max's coach. "There is nothing here for us."

"Not hardly," Max agreed, "but then it ain't for us

96

we're stopping. It's for them." He hooked a thumb in the direction of his horses.

"I want to go on. I do not like this place," Gilbert said.

"Fine."

"You agree then."

"Mister," Max said, "you can do whatever you want. I ain't holding you. But me and my coach are gonna stop here."

"So am I," Carl told him. "The horses need a break."

"If you want to walk on ahead, mister, you go right on an' do it," Max said.

Gilbert glared at Longarm. "Do something about this. Make them continue."

"Don't look at me. I got nothing to do with this."

The Frenchman did not look at all happy. Longarm gathered that the Marquis de Sant Cerre was not accustomed to disobedience from the working classes. He also gathered that Max and Carl were becoming fed up with Jean-Claude and his haughty manner.

"You fellas do whatever you want," Longarm said. "Me, I'm gonna go inside and see if I can scare up something to eat."

The proprietor of the crossroads store was a fat, grizzled old fart with a plump Mexican wife probably half his age and a flock of children swarming in and out. The house across the road belonged to them, and the kids fluttered back and forth, laughing and playing in the mud puddles. The storekeeper looked like a man who was contented with his life. Longarm admired that. Without wanting to imitate it, however.

"I don't serve meals. No call for it, if you see what I mean," the man said. He had given his name as Benjamin, which could have been his first name or his last, not that it mattered. "I have soda crackers here. Hardtack if you want something heavier. Pickled pig's feet and pickled sausages and pickled eggs. Canned peaches and canned tomatoes. You should be able to make a lunch from that, I'd think. And you're welcome to turn those horses into the pen over there. Fifty cents apiece for the hay and use of the fence."

"Fifty cents seems high to me," Max said.

Benjamin shrugged. "Suit yourself. Turn them loose in the brush if you don't want to pay. They can find some grass to pick at, probably some mesquite beans to eat. Do whatever pleases you."

"We will pay," Jean-Claude put in. He gave the man a gold coin. "That should take care of it. And of whatever we eat as well."

Benjamin examined the foreign coin and weighed it in his hand for a moment. Then he nodded. "Ayuh. This should cover you."

They ended up taking their lunch seated on crates at the back of the store, munching a little of this and a little of that.

"Any other parties of strangers come through lately headed westbound?" Longarm asked. He was thinking about whoever it was who was hunting for Jean-Claude. As slow as the wagons moved, there was the danger that the hunters could already be ahead and lying in wait.

"Friend, there's folks come through here every day. Some of them I know. Some of them I don't."

"The party I'm thinking of would be on horseback, not in coaches or wagons."

"How many in this bunch you're looking for?"

"I don't know," Longarm admitted. "Could be as few as one man or as many as . . . damn if I'd know."

"We don't get all that many horseback travelers passing through. It's easier to get a seat on a stagecoach. But we do see some once in a while. Had a party of three come by this morning. Can't tell you anything about them, though. They didn't stop at the store here, just rode by."

"Three men, you say?"

"That's right."

"How were they dressed? Cowhands, would you say?"

"Nope. These boys didn't look like they'd know one end of a cow from the other. I couldn't much tell how they was dressed. It was raining at the time, and they were covered all over with their slickers. But their hats were funny-looking things. Narrow brims, do you see. But not derbies. You see a derby now and then. These hats were kinda different from most. That's why I noticed them in particular was their hats."

"Were they armed?"

"I didn't pay any mind to that," Benjamin said. "And like I said, they were wearing slickers over their clothes. If they had rifles on their saddles or not . . . I couldn't say. Didn't think to look."

"All right, thanks."

Longarm chewed on a piece of spicy pickled sausage and pondered. Those riders were probably just businessmen going about their own affairs.

But they could also be someone with an unhealthy interest in Jean-Claude Gilbert and that piece of paper he carried with him.

Not that there was anything Longarm could do about it except press on and be vigilant while he did so.

If somebody wanted to make another try for Gilbert— or another attempt to kill Longarm—there was nothing to do but make sure they failed in their efforts.

Longarm would dearly love to find out who it was, though. And why. He would much rather go on the hunt for them than passively wait to be attacked.

He finished the sausage and reached for a pickled egg. Lucky for him that he liked the stuff.

Once the road began to dry out, they were able to make much better time, but the layover took up almost the entire afternoon, so their progress for the day was meager despite the fact that Gilbert insisted on pressing forward until they found an inn where he could have a room and a proper bed.

It was well past dark, and Longarm was more than ready for a hot meal and a bed of his own, before they finally stopped for the night. A bed, he intended, that would be shared by no one. He was still so worn out from the night before that it would have taken Lily Langtry *and* the Queen of Sheba to tempt him. And even then, he might just have rolled over and gone to sleep between them.

Gilbert booked rooms for himself and for Longarm but, apparently angry about the layover to allow the horses some rest, made no provision for either Max Dain or Carl Bonner.

"Be here at dawn. Prompt," he ordered them after the bags containing his immediate needs—which amounted to about half the wagon load—were carried upstairs.

Dain rolled his eyes and made a sour face in Carl Bonner's direction. Hell, Longarm understood why. It was one thing for Jean-Claude to issue instructions that they be ready to roll on at the break of dawn. But all of them, the drivers and Longarm too, knew good and well the Frenchman would not stir himself until he'd had his breakfast. They would be lucky to get on the road before eight o'clock regardless of what time Max and Carl presented themselves.

"See you in the morning, fellas," Longarm said as he made his way rather wearily to his room.

He slept extremely well on a bed that was unusually comfortable—or else Longarm was unusually tired—and woke feeling refreshed and ready. By the time Longarm shaved and shat, it was well past daybreak.

Jean-Claude's door was standing open when Longarm left his room, and for a moment he felt a chill of alarm at the thought that the arrogant marquis had come to harm while Longarm was next door snoring. As it turned out, the reason was a simpler one. A pair of very buxom young women were just then taking their leave from Jean-Claude. They came fluttering out into the hall and hurried down the back stairs, clutching their handbags tight in their hands. Longarm gathered that the Frenchman could be a generous soul when he was pleased by a, um, service.

"Good morning," Longarm said when Jean-Claude followed the women out of his room.

"Yes. Very good. Yes. Where are those stupid drivers? My things are ready to be taken down."

"I'm sure they're downstairs waiting by now," Longarm said. He dragged his Ingersoll from his vest pocket and checked the time. It was half past seven. "We can go ahead an' get our breakfast," he suggested. "I'm sure they'll have it taken care of by the time we're done."

Gilbert grumbled but agreed. There was no food service provided in the hotel, so they had to walk across the street to a small restaurant for a breakfast of pork chops, fried potatoes, and coffee.

There was no sign of the coach and wagon outside, but Longarm refrained from commenting about that.

Nor had the rigs been brought around to the front of the hotel by the time they were done eating.

Of course Max and Carl could have found it easier to load at the back of the tall hotel. Maybe.

They hadn't, and by eight forty-five they still had not turned up. Longarm checked with the desk clerk to see where a man might take a wagon and team for the night.

Neither Max nor Carl was at the wagon park, and there was no sign of their rigs either.

"Sure, they stayed here," a hostler at the nearby livery told him when Longarm inquired. "Nice fellas. Slept in the loft there. They pulled out, oh, three o'clock maybe."

"Headed east?" Longarm asked.

The hostler nodded. "That's right. Said they was anxious to get on home."

"Did they leave anything here? Some of their load, for instance?"

"Nope. The coach was empty when they left. The wagon was carrying a short load."

Longarm guessed they damn well must have been anxious because he knew for a fact that neither of them had yet been paid the wages Jean-Claude owed them for their services.

He wondered . . . hell, there was no accounting for what a man might take a notion to do, that was all.

But he suspected Jean-Claude was not going to like learning that so much of his traveling gear was gone. Including the cases of wine and cognac he'd brought. Now that, Longarm thought, was really going to piss him off.

Longarm headed back to the hotel to deliver the bad news.

Chapter 22

Longarm was not sure how old Jean-Claude Gilbert was. Somewhere in his thirties would have been Longarm's guess. Certainly he seemed too young to have a heart stroke. But he certainly looked like he might very well have one when Longarm told him about Max's and Carl's desertion.

The man screamed. He cursed—in French, but Longarm did not really have to comprehend the exact words; the sentiments were quite clear enough without that. He turned shades of red and purple. His eyes bulged from their sockets. Longarm would not have been greatly surprised to see smoke and steam spewing from his ears.

He was, Longarm suspected, pretty well peeved.

It took him half an hour to calm down, and then the calm was only relative.

"They must be found. Arrested. *Non!* They must be flogged. See to this, m'sieur. I demand it."

Longarm calmly lighted a cheroot and waited for the storm to subside. When finally it did, he asked, "Do I assume you still want t' go on?"

Gilbert looked at him as if Longarm had suddenly gone

daft. "Go on? But of course we go on, m'sieur. I have my duty to perform. As do you, *non*?"

"As do I, yes," Longarm agreed. "So. D'you want to hire horses or book seats on the next stagecoach? Either way, Jean-Claude, you're gonna have to leave most of your stuff behind. What's left of it."

"But—"

"Oh, don't give me no bullshit. None of that crap is essential, and even on a stagecoach there won't be room for everything. So which is it t' be, coach or horseback?"

"We will ride the coach, m'sieur." He said it, but it was plain to hear in his voice that he didn't like it. Hell, he'd be expected to travel like a regular human person instead of the Marquis de Sant Cerre. What a comedown. Or so Longarm suspected it would be from the Frenchman's point of view.

"I'll go find out about the schedule an' get our tickets."

"You will need money. Here." Jean-Claude produced a handful of gold coins and handed them over without bothering to count them. Longarm wondered what it must feel like to be that rich. Not that he would ever know. Nor, for that matter, that he cared all that much. There were other things that were more important. But it was something Longarm would've been willing to try.

"I won't be long," he said, and left the hotel in search of the local express agent.

Two hours later—and a good six hundred pounds of superfluous baggage lighter—they were on the road again, this time in the company of a drunk, a drummer, and two brassy young women who dressed like ladies but whose high-smelling perfume gave them away as whores.

Jean-Claude appropriated a seat between the women, and soon had them giggling and squirming.

Longarm tugged his hat brim low and tried to ignore the goings-on in the seat across from his.

• • •

The coach was a light one, built along the lines of an ambulance rather than the much heavier Studebakers or Concords, and was pulled by a six-up of small but exceedingly tough little Spanish mules. The driver kept them in a canter for a solid two hours—possibly because of the weight of the rig and the fact that the land here was so flat, with no uphill grades to conquer—until they reached the next relay station.

Transportation would be quicker and smoother once the railroads reached this part of the country. But as it was, the coach was averaging something on the order of ten miles each hour, Longarm calculated. The little mules were drenched in sweat and heaving for breath by the time they pulled into the station. They had damn sure earned their rest. Tomorrow, he supposed, they would turn around and make the same trip back the other way.

"We'll be here twenty minutes or so," the jehu announced from atop his driving box. "The facilities is out behind the store. There should be coffee and chili inside. There's liquor available through that door on the left if any of you gentlemen wants. And anybody that doesn't get on when I holler we're going can wait for the next coach west." Two Mexican boys were already busy unhooking the mules from their traces and leading them off to a small corral where water and hay were waiting.

That was one of the advantages of using the mules, Longarm realized. Horses would have to be watched over and kept apart from the water after a run like these little fellows just made, for an overheated horse would drink and eat until it foundered. A mule would regulate its own intake so as not to hurt itself.

Longarm stepped down out of the coach and waited for Jean-Claude, who was engaged in a sad good-bye to the two whores. It seemed this was their destination, although whether they were changing to another coach here or intended to stay here and work was unclear. Not that Longarm particularly cared, but Jean-Claude certainly seemed to. No doubt he'd been planning a night of revelry with the two busty women.

Jean-Claude's outlook brightened considerably about fifteen minutes later when he and Longarm emerged from the saloon side of the relay station to discover there was a new passenger who would be traveling on with them from here.

She was young, nicely dressed, and very pretty. She had a delicate neck, dark Latin features, and sparkling green eyes. When she climbed into the coach—Jean-Claude outran Longarm for the privilege of helping her up—her skirt hem lifted enough to show a slender and very shapely ankle concealed beneath white stockings.

Longarm felt a rise of sap in his crotch at the sight of the pretty young thing. She was, he guessed, twenty or thereabouts.

She also, dammit, seemed to be smitten with Jean-Claude Gilbert, the handsome son of a bitch.

But then, it was obvious from both his clothing and his demeanor that he was a rich and high-born dandy. Most women reacted to that like a kitten to catnip. Longarm was fairly sure if he'd been close enough, he could have heard this one purring already.

"My name is Genevieve du Charme," he heard her say. In a French accent, no less.

That tore it. There was no way Longarm would be getting a word in edgewise from here on, because Jean-Claude immediately launched into a torrent of liquid French. Miss du Charme answered in kind, and Longarm doubted either of those two was so much as aware of the existence of anyone else afterward.

Longarm crawled glumly into the coach. The drummer was already there.

"All aboard. We're rolling. If you ain't with me now, you ain't gonna be," the driver announced.

The drunk was still in the saloon propping up the bar, although whether he'd intended to stop here or not, Longarm neither knew nor cared.

The driver cracked his whip in the air above the leaders' ears, and the light coach snapped into motion, this fresh team jumping instantly into that swift and steady road canter.

Longarm looked at the drummer, then across toward Jean-Claude and Miss du Charme. The drummer smiled a little and shrugged, and Longarm grinned back at him in return. Nothing more needed to be said.

Once again Longarm tilted his Stetson over his eyes and settled in to wait as the team of mules carried them quickly along.

Chapter 23

"Whoa! Whoa up there, boys." The coach dragged to a jarringly sudden halt, bringing Longarm awake, "Whoa now."

Longarm stifled a yawn, his jaw shuddering and his neck muscles tightening. He rolled his shoulders and shook his head.

Gilbert and Miss du Charme had shut up and were leaning forward, heads intimately close together, to peer out the left side window.

"What's this?" Longarm asked the drummer, who had a watch in his hand and a puzzled look on his face.

The man shook his head. "Damn if I know. We aren't scheduled to stop for another half hour or so."

The driver's voice clarified the problem. "Don't shoot, mister. We aren't carrying any strongbox nor anything worth anybody getting shot over."

Longarm sighed. A holdup. Well, this just was not the poor bastard's day, deciding to rob a stage that happened to have a deputy U.S. marshal on board.

He drew his Colt and touched Jean-Claude on the shoulder. "Excuse me for a minute. I need to get to that window."

Jean-Claude settled back into his seat. Miss du Charme gave Longarm a startled look, then she too got out of his way.

Longarm crouched in the narrow gap between the seats and looked out. A single masked horseman was beside the front of the coach. He had the reins of a pair of spare horses in one hand and a sawed-off shotgun in the other. Longarm did not like the looks of that shotgun. One involuntary jerk on the trigger and somebody could get hurt. And where were the jaspers who belonged to those other horses? He didn't see them.

He leaned closer to the window, his Colt at the ready. If the robbers . . .

Longarm heard a dull, melonlike thump, very loud inside his head.

At the same time he felt a harsh impact on the back of his skull.

He had a dim and fleeting impression. A glimpse of the coach ceiling. A face, small and pale, above him. And a light, exceedingly pleasant sensation as if he were floating, drifting on the air like dust motes in sunlight.

Then he felt nothing at all.

Longarm felt like he'd been hit in the back of the head with an ax. And the damn thing was still there.

He tried to sit up. Big mistake.

Worse, when he slumped back down again, he bumped his head on the ground, which felt like the ax-whacker was hitting him all over again. Lordy!

"Lay still, mister."

He hadn't been aware until then that he was not alone. He managed to focus his eyes. Had to struggle some to do even that small thing. But he managed. The stagecoach driver and another man—oh, yes, the drummer; he remembered now—were kneeling beside him. And he was outside the coach, stretched out on the ground. He had no recollection of getting there, but suspected the two men must have pulled him outside. Likely they'd thought he was dying or already dead.

"Where . . . what happened?"

"It was that Frenchified female that hit you," the drummer said. "The little bitch had a cosh in her sleeve. Can you believe that? Had one of those long, leather ones filled real full of lead shot or some such. When you were looking out the window at that holdup man, she took as hard a swing at you as if she had a wood bat in her hands and was trying to smack a home run."

"From the way this feels, I'd say I'm damn lucky she didn't send my head flying over a fence," Longarm moaned.

"She could've killed you. In fact, me and Jim here thought she had done. I wouldn't be surprised if she didn't think so too."

"One of the few benefits of being hardheaded, eh?" Longarm said.

"If you can make light of it like that, friend, I expect you'll live."

"My gun. Where's my revolver?" Longarm asked, his fingers fumbling at his waist but finding only an empty holster there.

"She grabbed that up and held it on the man to make him go with her."

"Oh, shit!" Longarm grumbled. "He's been kidnapped?"

"He didn't go willing, I can tell you that much. She practically shoved that pistol inside his nose. Swore she'd shoot. Then the holdup man came around to the side of the coach and waved the shotgun at the Frenchman. That decided it."

"They didn't rob you?"

"Nope. Once the rig was stopped, neither of them paid any mind to us. The fella with the shotgun prodded you

110

in the ass with the muzzles. Acted like he was gonna shoot, but he never. I expect he thought you was dead too. You sure didn't react. But why'd he do that? Why'd he poke you in the butt like that?"

"It's a sure test to see if an animal . . . or a man . . . is playing possum. Nobody can resist tightening up his butt muscles if somebody pokes him in the asshole. If the cheeks stay loose, he's either out cold or he's dead, no two ways about it, because if he's the least bit awake you can feel the resistance in those muscles. It's a trick a hunter might know. And it keeps him out of the way, like in case a buck deer is knocked down and you don't know it it's dead. Prod it from in front, it may jump up and ram its antlers into your belly. Jig it in the ass with your boot, you'll know for sure and be out of the way if it does come onto its feet."

"I never knew that."

Longarm felt sick to his stomach. That was more than an aftermath of the blow he'd taken. He was also sick at the thought that he'd gone and lost the Marquis de Sant Cerre.

Billy Vail was not real apt to like this. Neither would the Attorney General nor the Secretary of State nor anybody in the whole damn government of France.

Custis old boy, he told himself, you've gone and fucked up pretty good this time.

"Help me up, would you? I got to . . ." He shut his mouth. He'd been about to say something about getting after the kidnappers.

Right.

No horse. No gun. And dizzy as a cuckoo bird swimming in a whiskey barrel.

The truth was that he was going to have to put himself back together before he could even think about getting Jean-Claude back from whoever those sons of bitches— and daughters of same—were.

111

Chapter 24

The next town up the line was a flyspeck on the map called Mule Ear. Mule Turd would have described it better. It had a couple stores, a couple saloons, a couple houses, and a couple people in it. Well, maybe a little more than that. But not much.

The stage stop was a many-functioned general store that sold a little of everything, contained the Post Office, and had a telegraph key along with a sign saying the telegraph was open for business between the hours of 9 and 11 A.M. only. The word "only" was underlined with three bold slashes of dark charcoal. It was now—Longarm checked his pocket watch—4:37 in the afternoon.

Longarm gave profuse thanks to the stagecoach driver and the drummer, then dropped his bag and Winchester onto the sagging porch outside the general store and entered.

"I need to send a telegram," he told the clerk inside the place.

"Yes, sir. You can write it out now if you like, but it won't go out till tomorrow morning."

"Mister, I don't like to disturb any man's routines, but this is official United States government business. I expect the message should go out now."

"Very well, sir, but as you can plainly see"—he pointed to the sign—"the telegraph office is only open mornings."

"I see that, friend, but today you are gonna make an exception."

"Mister, I don't know if you're deaf or stupid, but I already told you. No message until tomorrow. There won't be an operator here until then."

Longarm suspected the officious little prick was lying. He looked like the sort who would. But he had no way to prove that.

Longarm smiled at him. "That's no problem, friend. I'll send it my own self."

"You are not an authorized. . . ."

Longarm's patience was none too strong to begin with. And what little he possessed had been worn thin this afternoon. Being hit on the head and left for dead sometimes had that effect on him, which was probably a character flaw, but piss on the son of a bitch who wanted to say so.

Still smiling, he reached across the store counter that separated him from the store clerk. He took the man by the necktie and dragged him across the counter until the two were nose to nose.

"Friend," Longarm said, making a great effort to keep his voice calm and level, "friend, I have business to take care of here. And I am in a hurry. One man's life is already hanging in the balance here, and if you don't settle your ass down and take care of what I need, we are gonna have to add *your* life to that danger list. Or anyhow your liberty, because as God is my witness, mister, I will put you in handcuffs and ship you off to fucking Denver on charges of obstruction of justice, and you will sit your ass in a jail cell up there until I personally come to see to the disposition of your case. Am I making myself real clear now? Is there any part of this you would like me to repeat?"

"I think . . . I think . . ."

113

"Yeah. I thought you would." Longarm let go of the tie and pushed the man back upright.

He walked into the mail cage, where the telegraph key was, and poked around until he found the connections, hooked the set up, and tapped out a call signal. It was instantly returned by an operator somewhere up the line.

Longarm identified himself on the line and transmitted a brief report—as brief as he thought he could get away with—addressed to Billy Vail back home in Denver, along with an instruction that the message be copied to Department of State in Washington.

"You, uh, you were serious about this being official stuff, weren't you?" the store clerk commented.

"Read code, do you?"

"Yes, sir, I do." The man looked contrite. "I, um . . . you'd be surprised how many people . . . that is to say . . ."

"Forget it," Longarm told him. "It's just your bad luck I'm having a shitty day. I'm not always this testy."

"Yes, sir. I'm sorry."

"Look, I'm needing some things here. I'll pay with a voucher."

"That's fine, sir."

"First off, I need a gun. A double-action Colt if you have one."

"No such. I got a Smith & Wesson in .44 Russian caliber. It's used but in good shape. I got a couple new Remington revolvers in .44-40. No Colts in stock, though. I had one, but a fella bought it, oh, a couple or three months ago."

"I'll take one of the Remingtons," Longarm told him. He did not particularly like the Remington single-action, but at least that would carry the same cartridges as his Winchester saddle carbine. "The shorter barrel if there's a choice."

"Yes, sir." The clerk produced a standard .44 Remington six-gun with a four-inch barrel. Longarm thought them ugly, although not as butt-ugly as the Smith & Wessons were, but it would fit into his holster. More or less.

His leather had been custom-fitted to his own revolver. Damn that girl anyhow.

"A box of cartridges for it," he said. "No, make that four. I'll need to shoot this thing some to get the feel of it in my hand. Saddlebags. Ready-ground coffee and a camp pot. Cheese. Hard crackers. Dried beef. You got dried beef here?"

"Yes, sir. It's kind of peppery, though."

"That's fine. It will be light to carry and won't spoil. What else?" he mused aloud.

"Canned sardines?" the clerk suggested.

"That sounds good. Couple boxes of matches. Couple blankets. Slicker." He should have brought his saddle and traveling gear, dammit. "Folding camp saw if you have one."

"No, but I have a machete that's good and heavy. You could chop your firewood with that."

"I'll take it. Rubberized ground cloth. Picket rope. Oh, shit, what else?"

"You're wanting a horse, are you?"

"Yes, of course."

"Then you'd best hurry down the street if you want to catch Eddie Edwards at the barn there. He's due to lock up in a few minutes, and he hates to be bothered after hours worse 'n I do. You go on and take care of that. I'll get a pack of things ready for you here and have it waiting when you get back."

Longarm paused for a moment to reassess the fellow. "You're being mighty helpful, and I thank you."

"Yes, sir. Glad to do it."

Longarm nodded and hurried out to catch this Eddie person. Started off in a hurry anyway. He trotted about six yards before a renewed pounding in his head told him he was not yet ready for that. He slowed his pace, and after that had no problem.

And Eddie was still there, still open for business.

Damn those people anyway, though.

Chapter 25

Longarm figured he had two courses of action to choose between. He could go back to the spot where the stage was stopped and track the kidnappers from there. Or he could go directly to the place where they would surely be going, Gros Teton.

The choice was not as easy to make as first thought might suggest. Gros Teton, presumably the one here in Texas at least to begin with, was the easy answer. If the kidnappers were after the gold—and he knew of no other reason why they might want to capture the marquis and that document he was carrying—Longarm could go straight to their destination. Perhaps even get there ahead of them.

When he did, he might or might not recognize the man who'd had the shotgun. After all, Longarm had only caught a glimpse of him before the girl whacked him with her cosh. But he would most certainly know that damned Genevieve du Charme the next time he saw her, and girl or no girl, she was going to have some new bracelets, steel ones, as soon as he found her.

When he found her.

He sat mulling over his situation while at the same time

116

having what could prove to be the last hot meal he would have time for until Jean-Claude was recovered from the kidnappers.

He could go straight to Gros Teton, yes. But if he did that, it would leave Jean-Claude to the mercies, if any, of the people who'd snatched him.

Longarm had no doubt that the kidnappers would get the information they sought from Gilbert. They would force him to tell them, or they would find the instructions left by that survivor of the failed delivery to Maximillian. Either way, they would make their way to Gros Teton sooner or later.

If, however, they forced the information out of Jean-Claude, the Frenchman might or might not be alive to complete the trek to Gros Teton. And Longarm's duty lay in protecting the Marquis de Sant Cerre, not those chests of lost gold. Billy hadn't told him to get the gold back for the French. He'd said to escort Gilbert.

Which, so far, Longarm felt he was doing a piss-poor job of.

Hell, Jean-Claude could already be dead by now. The kidnappers already'd had several hours to work on him, and Longarm had no illusions about their ruthlessness. Anyone who was willing to murder a deputy United States marshal and thereby bring the full weight of the U.S. government down on themselves would not be squeamish about a little torture or maiming.

If he headed straight for Gros Teton, he would be as much as abandoning Jean-Claude to them.

But if he tried to go back and begin the process of tracking them from the ambush site, he would lose a good eighteen to twenty hours. Perhaps more, since it was now almost dark. Even if he could find the site in the dark, he would not be able to begin tracking them until daybreak. Plus that would put him back in the wrong direction by a dozen miles or more.

Dammit anyway, he silently groaned. Dammit.

If he went back, he ran the risk of losing them altogether. If he went on, he ran the risk of catching the kidnappers but losing Jean-Claude.

He was *not* going to lose those kidnappers, damn them.

He finished his supper, then went out to the tall, barrel-chested blue roan he'd bought from Eddie Edwards. It was time to get on the road. The horse was fresh, so there was no reason he couldn't put three or four hours behind him before he stopped for the night.

"No, sir, I haven't seen any strangers come through here in, oh, at least this past week. Well, except for the medicine show. There was a medicine show come through yesterday."

"Thanks. Say, you don't know where I could buy some .44 cartridges, do you?" He'd been burning them up for the past day and a half, practicing with the Remington at nearly every stop he made until by now he was becoming familiar with the feel of the revolver. It was not his tried-and-true Colt, and he didn't feel that it came out of the leather as easily as his own gun did. But it would do.

"Over yonder," the gent in the sleeve garters said. "I think Johnny carries ammunition for other than shotguns. That's about all anybody hunts around here, though, is quail and doves. Not much call for rifles and such."

"I see. Thank you again for your help." Longarm turned back to the big roan and led it across the street toward the store the friendly gent indicated.

He cast a wary eye toward the sky, where clouds were gathering dark and tall to the west. The past few days had been free of rain, and he hoped it would stay that way.

He entered the shop—it was barely large enough to be considered a business establishment at all—and greeted a man seated on what looked like a bar stool, although there was no bar anywhere in sight.

"What can I do for you, neighbor?"

"Cartridges," Longarm said. "In .44-40. Got any?"

"Got three boxes, I think."

"I'll take them."

"How many?"

"All three."

The storekeeper gave him a suspicious look, obviously wondering whether this stranger might be up to no good.

"New gun," Longarm explained. "I'm wanting to practice with it."

"Oh. Right." The fellow fetched out the three heavy, pasteboard boxes and handed them over. "Four dollars and a half," he said.

"Isn't that a little dear?" Longarm complained.

"If you don't want them, just hand them back. Makes no difference to me."

"I'll take them. I was just commenting." While Longarm was digging in his pockets for the money he took a look around at the rest of the merchandise. Most of it consisted of bottles, tins, and jars of patent medicines, stomach remedies, herbal tonics, cough syrups, laudanum, and the like. "I guess I could use a couple pounds of beans too if you have any," he added.

"Navy or pinto?"

"Pinto."

"Want some chilies to perk up the flavor? Maybe a chunk of bacon to throw in too?"

"You're a good salesman. Yes, I expect I'd take those too." Longarm reached inside his coat and, reminded, said, "How about cigars? I favor cheroots, the darker the leaf the better."

"All I have are stogies, panatelas, and crooks. The stogies taste like hell; the panatelas are ten cents each and don't taste much better. The crooks are brandy-cured. They're a little sweet, but the best of the lot. Penny apiece."

119

"Then I'll take a handful of those too."

The storekeeper got busy putting the order together, helpfully wrapping everything in brown paper tied off with string.

"Just out of curiosity," Longarm said, "do those traveling medicine shows hurt your business any?"

"Generally do," the man admitted, "but not for long. Two or three days and everything is back to normal."

"There must be good profit in medicines like that."

"Matter of fact, there is. Those traveling shows, they mostly make up their own infusions. Paste a fancy label on and sell for a dollar what it cost them a dime to make. And that includes the bottle. Sometimes I think I oughta buy myself a wagon and go on the road. Might be interesting."

"I'm sure it would be," Longarm said, meaning not a word of it. "But you have to have a show to draw the crowd, right?"

The storekeeper grinned. "I could paint my old lady brown and put a grass skirt on her. Let her jump around and holler like a wild Injun. If she showed a little leg, that oughta draw the crowd." He laughed. "Until the boys actually saw that leg. My old lady isn't what you'd call pretty."

"Good-looking woman with that outfit yesterday?" Longarm asked as he accepted his purchases and handed the storekeeper a ten-dollar eagle.

"I wouldn't know. They never stopped long enough to lay down their stage nor give us a show. Just bought some groceries and went on. Looking for bigger crowds than we could offer, I suppose."

"Yeah. Everywhere I stop I seem to be about half a day behind them. I'll have to catch up to them and get a look at what they have to offer. I've seen some mighty fine-looking girls working those wagons."

"Now that's the truth." The man counted out Longarm's change and wished him a good day.

Longarm was back outside, busy tying his new purchases into his bedroll, when it occurred to him that what he'd told that storekeeper was indeed the truth.

Yesterday, and now today too, wherever he went, wherever he asked about passing strangers, he was told about that medicine wagon.

They were always a matter of hours in front of him and moving west.

Without once stopping to make any sales.

It could well be, of course, that they were simply some honest folk—well, as honest as medicine peddlers are apt to be—hurrying on their way to a particular destination.

Or they could be someone who realizes that it isn't easy to hide a prisoner on a saddle, but you can damn sure conceal one inside a medicine wagon.

Longarm swung onto the saddle he'd bought to go along with the roan and pointed the horse's nose down the road to the west.

Chapter 26

He almost missed spotting them. The medicine wagon had been pulled into the shade of a stand on live oaks that straddled a shallow creek. It was only a wisp of smoke from a very nearly smokeless fire that gave them away.

It had taken him the remainder of yesterday and all this morning to catch up with them, but this had to be the outfit he was interested in. Once he realized they were there, he was able to make out some gold-leaf lettering on the side of the tall, narrow wagon. He made no attempt to approach them. Did not want to be recognized—if there were indeed the kidnappers—and maybe get something started at a time and place not of his own choosing. Instead, he rode on by as if he'd never seen the wagon there.

Likely someone over there was keeping an eye on the road, just in case. Longarm felt confident he would not be recognized. Not from this distance and mounted on a horse none of them would ever have seen.

Of course, he admitted to himself as he went on down the road, it was also entirely possible that the owner of that wagon over there was a genuine medicine show hustler with his little troupe, all of them stretched out in a patch of sweet grass to take a nap after the noon meal.

But he wasn't going to make that assumption.

He kept on at an easy road jog for a good half mile until the road took a southward curve and climbed over the top of a low rise. Once he was sure he was out of sight from the motte where the wagon was parked, he reined away to his right, toward the small stream that ran more or less parallel to the highway here.

The stream bank was hidden in dense brush, crackwillow and wild plum with elderberry bushes at the outer fringes. Longarm rode smack into the thicket and dismounted there, tying the roan securely instead of hobbling it and allowing it to browse the way he did when he was stopping to eat. He did not want the animal to wander out where it could be seen. Or, worse, get to feeling lonely and follow him downstream toward that medicine wagon.

Wouldn't that be a bitch. Find himself a nice spot where he could spy on the wagon, only to have the damn horse come along and nuzzle the back of his neck.

He'd had that happen once up in Montana. The horse came up on him so quiet, he never knew it was there until he felt it blow snot down his back. He almost came out of his skin that morning, and of course his spying game was ended right then and there. Fortunately, there hadn't been any real harm done that time. But he sure as hell didn't want a repeat of the experience.

He made sure the roan would stay put, then slipped his Winchester out of the saddle scabbard and began stalking slowly and silently along the creek.

He made his way as quietly as if he were intent on slipping up on a deer.

He didn't spook the people in the wagon.

Didn't get to spy on them either, dammit.

By the time he got down to where they had their nooning, they were already packed up and ready to roll out again.

The man on the driving box was a middle-aged fellow

with a paunch and blond hair. Longarm had never seen him before.

Beside him on the seat was a woman. She might well have been Genevieve du Charme. Or not. She was wearing a gingham dress and a pale-blue bonnet that drooped low over her face. From Longarm's angle, all he could see were the dress and the bonnet. He supposed those could have been worn by a big-ass monkey, and he wouldn't have known the difference.

The wagon was pulled by four light horses. But whether they were the same horses Longarm saw back there when the stagecoach was stopped . . . damned if he could recall. He'd been paying attention to the man with the shotgun, and that for only an instant. Then that treacherous du Charme bitch bludgeoned him and that was the end of that.

But they could be the same.

Or not.

The driver clucked his team into motion, and the medicine wagon rolled out. The gold lettering read PROFESSOR JONAS SOAMES, EMOLUMENTS AND INFUSIONS. Longarm kind of assumed whoever wrote that sign meant emollients. He didn't know what the hell an emolument was. If it was a word at all.

The wagon drove out to the road and turned west, leaving Longarm standing hidden in the bushes grumbling. He wished now the horse *had* followed him, damn it all anyway.

As it was, he had to walk a half mile back before he could start after that wagon again.

The wagon wasn't moving so fast that it was any trouble catching up with them again. Once he had them in sight and knew they wouldn't slip away onto a side road, he dropped back, giving them their head and biding his time.

Late in the afternoon, they reached a pleasant little

town—a sign on the outskirts said it was Haraldsville—with a decent-looking hotel and a public wagon park. The place looked big enough to bring in a good crowd for a medicine show. But not on this night. The wagon rolled right on through and out the other side, depriving the good folks of Haraldsville of their entertainment.

Longarm found that sorta curious. It certainly was not criminal, though. He continued to follow. But hoped they'd stop soon for the night. Because of the time he'd wasted trying to creep up on the wagon during their dinner hour, he hadn't had dinner of his own, and by now was becoming plenty hungry with only a cold and skimpy breakfast so far for the day.

The wagon kept on until nearly full dark before they finally turned off into a fenced pasture that had a windmill and water tank in it.

Longarm watched from a distance while someone got out of the back of the wagon to open the gate and allow the wagon through. Then he conscientiously closed the gate again, and stood on the wagon sideboard to ride the hundred yards or so from the roadway to the stock tank. Longarm wished he had field glasses with him so he could get a look at the man who'd been hidden inside the wagon all day.

The older fellow, who was driving, climbed down and helped the woman down while the man from inside the wagon went about the routine camp chores, unhitching the horses first and allowing them to drink, then putting them in hobbles and turning them loose to graze.

The door at the back of the wagon opened and yet another man came out. He began putting a fire together using what dry brush he could find and picking up some other fuel, which Longarm could not see but assumed would be dried cow patties. The woman took charge of the fire, and pretty soon the bunch of them had a nice and cozy little camp set up for the night.

125

Longarm stayed back where he was until it was good and dark. He gnawed on a little dried beef and washed it down with a swallow of tepid water from his canteen. He'd had better meals. Worse ones too.

Finally, while the folks in the wagon were engrossed in a somewhat finer meal than Longarm's had been, he tied the roan securely to a fence post, took his Winchester, and slipped through the barbed-wire strands to enter the pasture where the medicine wagon was parked.

It was time to see what was what with these people, he thought, while they were still awake, and he could take advantage of the light from their fire to look them over.

He began slowly and cautiously to creep up on them for the second time that day.

Chapter 27

"It's a waste o' damn time," one of the younger men grumbled.

"No!" the older one, the man who had been driving the wagon, told him. "We do not know. We wait. We may need this one." He had a French accent, Longarm noticed.

Longarm was lying not more than thirty feet away from the campfire, just on the shadow side of their wagon. It had taken some time, but he'd bellied in good and close. Close enough that he could smell their coffee. Damn, but he did wish he could have a cup of that.

The woman said something too, but Longarm had no idea what it was because she spoke in French. The man, who seemed to be in charge, responded, and the girl angrily shook her head. Longarm still could not see her face, dammit, but he was fairly sure she was Genevieve du Charme.

Above him, the wagon bed rocked a little, even though the team was not attached to it and the people seemed all to be sitting beside the fire. Then he heard a faint thump inside the wagon as well. He began to smile. Jean-Claude Gilbert, the Marquis de Sant Cerre? He would've bet the farm on that. If he had a farm. And someone to take the wager.

"Should I take him something to eat?" one of the hired

hands asked. He inclined his head in the direction of the wagon. Longarm was not sure, but suspected that he was the one who'd stopped the stagecoach. There was no sign of his shotgun now, but both Americans were wearing revolvers. The Frenchman or the girl could have been hiding a dozen pistols in their clothes and Longarm would have no way to know it. He could not see any weapon on them, though.

Obviously, he thought, Jean-Claude was still alive and was being held inside the wagon. Good.

"Yes. Take him one of these . . . whatever you call these execrable things," the leader said. He peeled a strip of fire-baked bread off the stick it was wrapped around and handed it to the man who'd offered to feed Jean-Claude. "But no coffee. He could throw it on you, *non*? Hot. Give him only water to drink."

"He ain't gonna try anything, Louie. Not with me. I'll bust his face in."

"Do what I say. Water only, no coffee."

"Yes, sir." The hired hand sounded disappointed that Jean-Claude would have no opportunity to act up.

The fellow stood and brushed off the seat of his britches. The other one stirred. "Want some help, Bud?"

"No, thanks. Set where you are."

The one called Bud began walking toward the wagon.

Perfect, Longarm thought. He slithered silently to his right, close to the ground. When he got behind the rear wagon wheel, he rose into a crouch, paused for a moment, and then leaned the Winchester against the axle where it could quickly be grabbed if he needed it.

Bud reached the back of the wagon and planted a boot onto the steel step beneath the narrow door.

Longarm came to his feet and stepped forward, placing himself behind Bud.

He had the heavy Remington in his fist. Lifted it and gave Bud a solid whack on the back of the head using the flat of the pistol butt to strike him. He'd seen lawmen stun arrested parties with the barrels of their revolvers. He'd also seen those barrels bent slightly out of true as a result of that abuse. Better to use the butt, he figured.

Bud collapsed, falling backward into Longarm's grasp.

Longarm dragged the limp body behind the wagon and stretched him out on the ground there, then returned to the wagon entry.

In a low and cautious whisper he asked, "Jean-Claude?"

"Who . . . ?"

"Keep your voice down, dammit."

"Long?" This time Jean-Claude spoke in a barely audible whisper also.

"Yeah, it's me."

"I thought you were dead."

"Well, damn, Jean-Claude, you don't have t' sound so damn disappointed to learn you was wrong."

"To the contrary, I am quite pleased." While they were whispering, Jean-Claude was busy scooting on his ass across the floor of the wagon to the back door. He was bound hand and foot.

"Hold still." Longarm stuffed the Remington back into his holster and dipped into his pocket for his knife. He flicked it open and quickly sliced through Jean-Claude's bonds.

"Ah, that feels better." Jean-Claude began vigorously rubbing his wrists. "Give me a gun. I will help you to arrest these people."

"Right."

Longarm had no firearms to spare, but Bud did. Longarm found the supine figure, and bent over it in order to retrieve Bud's revolver.

He leaned down.

He received a kick in the side of his jaw.

Bud shouted a warning as Longarm reeled backward from the force of the unexpected blow.

129

"Prisoner's loose!" the hired man roared. He bounced to his feet, silhouetting himself against the firelight.

Bud grabbed for his pistol.

Over by the fire there was a commotion, shouting and cursing in at least two languages. They were alerted, all right.

Not that Longarm had time to worry about them right now. Bud was the immediate threat. His Colt was clearing leather—but not quickly enough from his perspective—when Longarm palmed his own gun. He remembered to thumb back the hammer of the single-action Remington, and triggered a round into Bud's chest from no more than four feet away.

The effect was instantaneous. Bud's knees buckled and he toppled face-forward onto the ground.

Longarm stepped sideways, Remington held ready for a second shot.

There was no one there to shoot at.

The circle of firelight was empty. There was no sign at all now of the two men and the woman who only moments ago were there enjoying their supper.

The three of them might as well have evaporated into the night like a wisp of fog blown away by a vagrant breeze.

"Shit! Get down, Jean-Claude."

Jean-Claude had been about to emerge from the wagon. Instead of dropping to the ground now, he threw himself backward into the wagon.

Longarm took his own good advice and dropped belly-down an instant before the bright fireball of a muzzle flash lit up the side of the water tank.

Longarm snapped two answering rounds toward the spot where the shot came from, then quickly rolled to his left, behind the wagon wheel. The wheel might offer scant protection. But then scant is better than none.

He lay silently then. Waiting. The only sound came from the crackle of a dying fire.

It was a very long time before he moved again.

Chapter 28

"They're gone," he announced in a normal voice that sounded unnaturally loud in the darkness now.

"You are certain?"

"Yeah. I've crept circles around this spot four times now. If there was anybody out there, I'd 've found them. They've vamoosed."

"They have . . . what is this word?" Jean-Claude asked. Longarm noticed that the Frenchman still hadn't emerged from the protection of the wagon.

"Gone. Out o' here. Scampered. Skeedaddled. Jean-Claude, they ain't here no more. I guarantee it."

"But we will not take chances, no?"

"We will not take chances. No," Longarm agreed.

Gilbert finally poked his head out of the back of the medicine wagon and looked carefully around, never mind that the night was overcast and moonless, before stepping down to the ground.

"You don't look too awful bad for a man that's been tortured for information," Longarm observed aloud.

"Torture? Why would I subject myself to this abuse, eh? I am not tortured." Jean-Claude walked over to the

131

red glowing embers of his captors' fire and helped himself to a skillet containing a hash of some sort.

"I just naturally thought they'd beat the information out of you," Longarm said, reaching for a spoon and helping himself to some of the chuck too. It beat the hell out of a piece of jerky and a swig of lukewarm water.

"That would be barbaric," Jean-Claude retorted. "I am a realist, no? So is Louis." He pronounced it with the emphasis on the latter syllable. Jean-Claude shrugged. "He explained to me my"—he paused, searching for the word he wanted—"my alternative. I could speak with him. I could suffer. The choice he lef' to me. I do not wish to suffer. So I tell him. I tell him we go to Gros Teton. I do not say to *which* Gros Teton we go."

"Jean-Claude, you don't know yourself which Gros Teton the instruction means," Longarm reminded him.

"And now Louis does not know this too," Jean-Claude said with smug satisfaction.

"Just what did you expect to do once you got there?"

"But I wait for you to come, m'sieur. This is why you are here, no?"

"I thought you thought I was dead," Longarm said.

"But no, m'sieur. I believe that silly girl, she think you are dead. Me, I know better. The dead man he falls so. He is . . . loose? No. Limp. He is limp as he falls. Falls hard like bag of meal dropped on the floor. You did not fall so. You were tense. Taut. You bounced when you struck that floor. So I know you will be along to help me. Knowing this, why should I allow those ruffians to do unpleasant things to me, eh? So . . . I tell Louis. We go to Gros Teton."

"And the directions to the treasure? Did you give them the paper?"

Jean-Claude laughed. "You see that this night I was tied and left in the wagon, no?"

"Yes, so?"

He laughed again. "Last night, Louis he tries to humble me, Jean-Claude Gilbert, Marquis de Sant Cerre, me. Ha! He tells me to build the fire. So . . . I build the fire, no?"

"So?"

Even in such poor light Jean-Claude's grin was visible in the white of his teeth. "So I need tinder to start the fire. Paper is good for this purpose, yes?"

Longarm laughed too. "The word map? You used the directions to make the fire?"

"*Oui*. It burned very nicely."

"But what about . . . ?"

"It is not to worry, Deputy of the Long Arm. I remember every word the sheet it says. Every one."

"I hope to hell you do."

"I assure you."

"All right then."

"The coffee, it smells so good. Do you see a cup I can use?"

Longarm found one for Jean-Claude and another for himself.

He was beginning to think the Frenchman . . . no, he wasn't beginning to think it. He was convinced of it. Jean-Claude Gilbert was one crazy son of a bitch. Still, crazy or not, his method had worked. He was safe from the kidnappers.

For now.

As for tomorrow, well, that remained to be seen.

Longarm helped himself to another cup of coffee, then hefted his Winchester and walked out into the darkness. There wouldn't be any sleep for him tonight lest Louis and that other son of a bitch decided to sneak back and make another try at them.

"Aw, shit!" Longarm grumbled aloud.

"What is it? What is wrong?" Jean-Claud jumped to the wagon door, the Remington revolver in his hand. Longarm had appropriated the dead kidnapper's Colt for himself and given the Remington to Jean-Claude. He just plain liked the feel of the Colt better, even the single-action-model Peacemaker like this one. He had no idea what had become of the little nickel-plated pistol Jean-Claude started out with.

"Look." Longarm pointed. The ground where the campfire had been last night was awash with muddy water.

"Yes?"

"When I shot back at those people last night, one o' my bullets must've hit the stock tank. Damn thing's been leaking all damn night. It must be about empty by now."

"Yes, well, it is a shame, I am sure. What about my breakfast?"

"If you're hungry, Jean-Claude, you can get your own damn breakfast. I got to go find some wood."

"Wood for the fire?"

"No, wood so's I can whittle a plug to stop up that bullet hole. Can't be letting cows go without water just because I missed what I was aiming at."

"But we cannot take the time. . . ."

Longarm wasn't listening. He was already busy looking for a piece of green wood of a good size to stop up a .44-caliber hole. He would fix the damn tank, then turn on the windmill-driven well pump before they left. He owed that much to whoever's ground this was.

Once he found what he wanted, Longarm whistled softly under his breath while he scraped and whittled to get the peg the exact right size.

Chapter 29

"Jean-Claude, you look like a new man."

"You mock me, m'sieur."

"Yes, I expect that I do at that." Longarm laughed. "But you really do look a completely different fella in those clothes."

"I look like a cowboy," Gilbert said in a voice that clearly turned the statement into a complaint.

"Oh, I wouldn't say you look that good, so don't be insulting to cowboys. But you do look like a normal person now that you're wearin' regular clothes."

The Frenchman mumbled a little under his breath, and Longarm laughed again.

Gilbert's luggage, pretty much everything he owned, had been either carted away by Max and Carl when they defected, abandoned back east when they switched onto the stagecoach . . . or left behind on the coach when Louis Mansard and company kidnapped him.

The persnickety Frenchman was miserable without fresh clothing to change into after his rescue, and insisted they stop at the next town so he could shop for clothing. He refused to consider the ready-made suits that were available, and ended up in corduroy and flannel. And a sour expression to go with them.

Longarm kinda thought he looked like a forester in his new duds. Or a hardware salesman.

Jean-Claude did seem to fancy the idea of wearing the big .44-40 Remington on his belt instead of having to hide it away. If he'd only bought himself a wide-brimmed hat, Longarm thought, he would develop a swagger and a Texas drawl.

Longarm burst out laughing.

"Yes? What is it?"

"Nothin'," Longarm lied, trying to swipe the smirk off his face. It was just that the thought of Jean-Claude Gilbert speaking in a slow drawl and that French accent both at the same time . . . that was too much to hold in.

"Is that everything?"

"Oui, m'sieur."

"Then we'd best be on the road. It wouldn't do for us to disappoint your friends up there waiting for us."

"Louis and Genevieve?"

"There's nobody else that I know about. Or is there something you haven't told me?"

Jean-Claude did not answer. But then he didn't have to. There was a hell of a lot that he had not disclosed to Longarm, and Longarm knew it. Longarm just hoped whatever those secrets were, they were not the sort of thing that was apt to get one of them—or both of them—killed.

Longarm picked up the hitching weights, unclipped them from the horses' bits, and dropped them onto the floor of the medicine wagon driving box. They had appropriated the wagon after Mansard and his friends abandoned it. As a precaution, Longarm was leaving the roan saddled during the day and tied at the tail end of the wagon, just in case Mansard and company made another try for Jean-Claude, and he needed to use it to give chase.

He really did not expect that, though. Mansard now knew where they were going. It only made sense for them to go ahead and wait for Jean-Claude to show up in Gros Teton.

"Y'know," Longarm mused out loud as they rolled westward, "we could maybe throw a clinker into their plans if we skip past Gros Teton, Texas, and look in New Mexico first."

"Non," Gilbert said firmly. "I look at the maps. This place we go to now, it is the one most likely to be what we seek. Gros Teton, New Mexico Territory, it is too far north and west for someone seeking to carry gold to Maximillian. I do not say this is impossible, no. But in Texas, this is the place that is likely."

"Whatever you say. I'm just the bodyguard. You go wherever you please."

"Merci."

Longarm reached into his coat and brought out a brandy crook; he was out of his favored cheroots, but the crooks were not all that bad. He offered the ugly little cigar to Jean-Claude, and was rewarded with a look of insulted distaste. The Marquis de Sant Cerre had not sunk that low. Yet. Longarm chuckled and lighted up.

"Gros Teton. That mean what I think it does?" Longarm asked.

Jean-Claude cupped his hands in front of his chest and said, *"Oui.* Big ones. Huge. What you call, I think, knockers."

"Yeah, I thought so, but I'm telling you, whoever named those molehills was so hard up for seein' a woman, he'd purely forgot what one looks like." He indicated the low mounds, neither of them more than fifty feet high, that lay on the shore of a dried-up lake bed.

"Gros Tet . . . this place is it? This is Gros Teton?"

"Ain't much, is it," Longarm agreed. "But it's the place, all right."

A sunbaked town that probably boasted a population of no more than a couple hundred, if that many, nestled at the base of the two rough and lumpy hills. Longarm could not help but wonder how the rocky outcroppings came to be here when everything around them was flat and featureless for a good dozen miles in any direction.

One thing for sure. No one was going to sneak up on Gros Teton, Texas. A horseman—hell, a man on foot— would be visible for miles before he ever reached the town limits. It was an ugly little burg, with virtually nothing to recommend it.

"Why would such a place exist, eh?" Perhaps Jean-Claude was having similar thoughts.

"Salt," Longarm said.

"Pardon?"

"You see that dry lake? Rainwater, what there is of it, which probably ain't much, collects there. Prob'ly flows here from the whole of a hundred square miles or more. Then it all evaporates away. There's no regular flow into the lake and none at all out of it. So the water sits there. When it's gone, it leaves behind whatever minerals it was carrying. See how pale it looks? That's salt.

"Folks been coming here since before us white men came onto the scene, back for hundreds an' hundreds of years, I'd guess. Maybe thousands. They come an' take the salt. So sometime ago some smart sonuvabitch filed on the land and started mining an' bagging it. That needed workers, men to dig the salt and others to dry it and more to haul it. The workers brought families with them. Then there had t' be stores to provide for their needs an' take their pay. An' some horny soul went an' named it Gros Teton."

He paused to take a final drag off the crook he was smoking, then tossed it down onto the hardpacked ground beside the road. "Now you know 'bout all there is t' know about Gros Teton, Texas."

"Yes. Except where Louis is."

"He's somewhere up ahead there, Jean-Claude. Count on it."

The Frenchman squared his shoulders and touched the butt of the Remington. He had been practicing with the .44-40 since Longarm gave it to him, and had developed into a more than passable shot. He was slow with the gun, and probably always would be no matter how much he practiced. But he was accurate. Longarm hoped that would be good enough if—when—the time came that he had to use the gun.

Longarm figured the one thing they had to their advantage in this deal was that Louis Mansard could not afford to kill Jean-Claude. Not with the cartograph burned up and gone.

All Longarm had to protect him against was another kidnapping. Not that he'd done all that splendid a job of things the last time around. But he knew the enemy better this time, and he was ready for their treachery.

He hoped.

He shook out his lines and clucked the team forward.

That fabled city of Gros Teton—misnamed though it was—awaited.

Chapter 30

Small though it was, Gros Teton had a hotel, probably relying on business from the freight wagons coming through to carry salt. There was also a large area surrounded by an adobe fence where horses and mules could be turned in.

"This," Jean-Claude declared, "is not a hotel."

"It's a two-bit flop where they cater to mule skinners," Longarm told him. "It's also the only place in town where we're apt t' find sleeping quarters."

Gilbert sniffed and looked down his nose at the offending establishment. Which, if the truth be told, was a mite on the offensive side. Had Longarm been alone—and not thinking in terms of someone maybe wanting to shoot him while he slept—he probably would have ridden right on through to sleep on the desert. As it was, well, beggars can't choose.

"One thing you oughta know," Longarm said as he climbed down off the medicine wagon. "They likely won't have private rooms. There might be a dozen or so beds all together. Don't get snotty about it, or we'll end up with no room tonight, and I don't fancy sleeping under the stars so long as Louis Mansard is around."

Gilbert looked quite perfectly scandalized, but he kept his mouth shut.

Longarm led the way inside. There was no reception desk or guest book, but there was a fellow in sleeve garters and a marvelously filthy shirt who presided over the lobby—which doubled as a saloon—from a corner table. A sign over the table said OFFICE, and he had a cash box on the table before him. A big old Walker Colt lay beside the cash box. The antique, Longarm saw, had been converted to cartridge use at some time in the past. If it ever was fired, it very well might blow up in the shooter's hand.

"There's two of us," Longarm told him. "Dunno how long we'll be staying."

"Fifty cents an' you'll share a bed," the proprietor said. "Over there." He pointed toward a blanket nailed over a doorway. "Stay as long as you like, but pay me once a day before you lay down. You got livestock?"

"We do."

"You can turn 'em loose in the pen yonder. No charge for that, but we don't provide fodder nor water. How many head you got?"

"Three."

The man nodded. "Quarter apiece for them too if you want to feed them some hay from the shed out back. There's a water trough there too. The price of the hay includes all the water they can drink. One armload o' hay for a quarter. If you take more, I'll know it and I'll be collecting from you." He patted the rusty cylinder of the outmoded old Colt. Longarm managed to avoid feeling menaced by the gesture.

"My good man," Jean-Claude put in, unable to contain himself any longer, "I shall require a room to myself. To say nothing of a bed of my own. And a bath, if you please."

"Mister, that's no problem a'tall."

Jean-Claude shot a triumphant I-told-you-so look toward Longarm.

"Straight ahead," the hotel proprietor went on. "You'll find everything you need over to El Paso. But if you stay here, it's two t' the bed. And mind you take your boots off before you crawl in. I don't want my blankets gettin' all muddy."

Jean-Claude looked mortified.

"Do you serve food too?" Longarm asked.

"I do. Fifteen cents apiece if you want to feed. Breakfast is on the house."

"We'll take supper too then," Longarm said, paying the man for their food and lodging plus hay for the horses. He paid it quickly from his own pocket to make sure Jean-Claude did not drag out a handful of gold to sort through. That would only invite trouble from more than Louis Mansard's crowd.

Come to think of it, Longarm wondered why Mansard had not bothered to rob Jean-Claude of his money belt when they had the Frenchman.

Money just did not seem to be of much importance to either side of this odd deal. And never mind their claims that they were trying to recover that shipment of French gold. There was something going on here apart from that. Longarm wished he knew what the hell it was.

They didn't have so much gear as to be a burden, not after losing virtually everything along the way. Longarm brought in the few things they would need come morning, and figured the rest would be as safe in the back of the medicine wagon as in the hotel dormitory.

Supper consisted of salt pork, half-raw biscuits, rice, and thick gravy. The gravy had lumps in it big enough to lame a mule, but the flavor was all right. Longarm had had worse meals.

After they ate, Longarm left Jean-Claude to his own devices in the hotel, telling him, "I want to get those horses bedded down before it gets too late."

Jean-Claude made no offer to help with the chores. Not that Longarm expected any.

He gathered up the three animals and led them around to the back of the hotel, dragged down three armloads of hay—it was actually a decent-quality hay, which he was more than a little surprised to discover—and tied them to a fence rail so they could eat at their own pace without having to compete with other animals in the public corral.

Longarm lighted a brandy crook and leaned against the back wall of the hotelier's shed, where he would not be an easy target just in case someone wanted to take an unhealthy interest in him.

"M'sieur." The voice was a throaty whisper coming from the front of the shed. A *female* throaty whisper.

Longarm slid to his right a little and laid his hand on the butt of the Colt at his belt.

"Do not be alarm, m'sieur," the whisper came again.

"What d'you want, Genevieve?"

He heard soft laughter. "You remember me, no?"

"I wish t' hell I didn't." Just thinking about it made the back of his head hurt all over again. "You got that cosh with you?"

"The . . . what, m'sieur?"

"Cosh. Bludgeon. That weighted thing you whacked me with."

"Oh. That," she said, sounding as if the incident was of no consequence. Maybe not to her anyway. "No, I come now just me. See?"

She stepped into sight in the open front side of the shed. She stood facing him, hands slightly extended away from her body.

There was little light in the evening sky, but there was enough that he could see she was wearing a simple shift now and not one of her fancy gowns.

"I am not armed," she said. "May I prove this?"

"If you want."

Genevieve du Charme smiled. And dropped the shift from her shoulders.

She was not wearing anything underneath it.

The girl had a body fit to make a man drool down his chin and bark at the moon. She had an impossibly narrow waist, delicate tip-tilted tits, and a heart-shaped swell of hip above slender thighs and shapely calves.

"See?" she said. "No firearms. No . . . cosh, is it? No weapons, m'sieur."

"How about in your hair?"

She reached up, the gesture doing lovely things to her breasts, and took her time unpinning her hair. She tossed her head from side to side to loosen it and send it cascading over her shoulders and halfway down her back.

She was gorgeous, no doubt about it.

"Louis send you here, did he?" Longarm asked.

"But of course, m'sieur. I am told to seduce you."

"Then what, kill me when I'm not expecting it?"

"M'sieur," she chided, sounding disappointed in him. "Please. I am not so . . . common as that."

"It's been tried before," he said, thinking back to the girl on the riverboat. She had been sent by Louis too. Or so he had to assume anyway.

"But not by me, m'sieur." She laughed. "If I wanted you dead, m'sieur, I would make your heart to fail from an excess of ecstasy. I could do this, I assure you."

"Damn if I don't think maybe you could, Genevieve."

"I am honest with you, m'sieur. I have come to seduce you. And to speak with you. Monsieur Mansard wishes to enlist you to his cause. I will explain to you why it is in your interest to do this thing."

"I already got my assignment, thanks."

"But m'sieur, it is in the interest of your country as well as mine. Will you not listen to me?" She drifted forward, naked and lovely, smiling, encouraging in a soft

144

and gentle voice the same way a man might gentle a half-broke filly with his tone of voice. "That is all I ask. Only listen. And, m'sieur, I will make you *very* happy while you listen, no?"

She reached him. Positioned herself so close that he could feel the warmth of her breath on his throat. Reached up with both hands and encircled his neck. Her skin was searingly hot and softer than any velvet.

"But later, m'sieur," she murmured, her lips brushing lightly against his as she drew his head down to her kiss. "We talk later. Later."

Longarm's erection like to ripped the buttons off his fly.

"Later," Genevieve whispered again.

She tasted of peppermint, and he could feel the tips of her breasts pressing soft and warm and insistent through the cloth of his shirt.

Almost as if he no longer had any control over his own flesh, Longarm wrapped his arms around the beautiful French siren.

He bent. Slipped an arm behind her knees and picked her up. She weighed little more than an armload of fodder.

He carried her four steps, and carefully lowered her onto a pile of soft, sweet smelling hay.

Genevieve moaned softly as the tip of her tongue began to probe the inside of Longarm's mouth.

She was beautiful. And she was eager.

And he was not a complete idiot simply due to the presence of a pretty girl. His eyes remained open and he kept his attention—a part of it anyway—on the open shed front. Just in case the lovely Miss du Charme was not alone.

145

Chapter 31

Longarm kissed the writhing, moaning, eager girl. He ran his hands through her hair. And checked to make sure nothing was concealed there.

While Genevieve fumbled his fly open, Longarm removed his gunbelt and prudently moved it out of her reach.

It was all he could do though to keep his attention where it belonged. Genevieve du Charme held nothing back.

She unfastened the buttons of his vest and his shirt and spread them open, not willing to waste the time it would take to fully remove them.

She kissed his jaw, his throat, ran her tongue across his chest, and paused to lick and suckle at each of Longarm's nipples.

Her hand clutched at his cock, kneading and pulling as if milking him.

"Slow down," he whispered, "or I'm gonna squirt all over your hand."

"Let me to take the edge off, *cher*." She pressed her lips tight around his shaft, pulling back against the suction she was creating, her tongue laving the engorged head one moment, roving over the tender skin of his balls the next.

He really had been ready to explode. Within seconds he came, the hot fluid gushing into her mouth.

Genevieve stayed there, sucking and swallowing until he was done. Then she smiled and shivered with pleasure. "Now," she said, "you will not be so quick. Now the turn it is mine."

With tongue and fingertips, she brought him back to a throbbing hardness, then rolled on top of him and with a practiced wiggle of her hips, encompassed him inside the moist heat of her sheath.

Longarm fondled her tits, squeezing and teasing her nipples while Genevieve rode him.

Within a few seconds her expression went slack as her attention focused on the sensations she was receiving. She closed her eyes and arched her back, head thrown back and the cords of her slender neck prominent. She began to tremble.

Longarm could feel the quivering movement reach him first in the flesh that engulfed his cock, then in the soft rich swells of her breasts. Her breath quickened, and she began to gasp.

Genevieve shuddered and cried out, her yelp of pleasure as sharp and piercing as a fox's bark.

She collapsed, falling forward onto his chest and lying there dead still and silent. He was not sure if she'd passed out or died.

She had said something about giving him heart failure through the intensity of her lovemaking? Apparently, that was a double-edged sword.

Not that he'd ever thought of his pecker as being a weapon. Exactly.

He stroked the long, smooth muscles in her back and felt the thumpety-bump of her heart beating rapidly against his chest.

A moment later, Genevieve opened her eyes. She

looked into his and smiled, then kissed him long and soft. He could taste himself and could smell the faint, seawater scent of his semen on her breath.

"Are you all right?" he asked.

"*Oui,*" she whispered. "You are . . . I did not expect . . . so big." She smiled again. "So ver' nice, no?"

"So very nice, yes," he agreed.

Genevieve ran her fingertips over his throat and onto his lips. She kissed him again and planted very soft butterfly kisses on his eyelids. "You are so much a man, Custis Long. Help me, will you?" Her eyelids fluttered quite becomingly. "Please?"

It was the thing with the eyelids that brought Longarm quite firmly back to earth. That was just a bit too, too much. Too artificial. Damned if the girl hadn't almost had him right up until then, though. She was good. Very good. A great fuck and a joy to look at. He sort of hated having to go back to work now.

"How can I help you?" he asked.

"But m'sieur, it is I who would help you," she said in that soft, sweet voice, laying her pretty head back onto his chest and sighing to emphasize the words.

"How's that?"

"This thing you seek. Everything you are told, it is a lie, m'sieur."

"Really?"

"*Oui,* this is true. The document proves the masters of Le Belle France to be false, m'sieur."

Document? He had no idea what document she was talking about. But he had no intention of telling her that.

"You do not speak French, m'sieur?"

"No, of course not."

"Then you do not read it too, *non*?"

"Nope. Don't speak it nor read it neither one."

"M'sieur, the document it is important. It is vital to the interests of your country and of mine."

"But you're French, right?"

"Certainment, m'sieur," she said indignantly. "I am a loyal daughter to this my country."

"The French ambassador asked for my government's help with this. He's the one who sent the marquis on this mission."

Genevieve mimed spitting. "Pah! The ambassador. That pig! He is a traitor to the true people of France. He is worse even than the monarchist Gilbert."

"Monarchist?"

"Oui, but of course. You did not know?"

"It isn't something that's ever come up in conversation," Longarm said.

"Pah!" She made as if to spit again. "But you will see. The document proves this. That is why we must have it. We must show the world the . . . the . . . the crimes of these people. There is another word in the English. I do not remember it. Perflu . . . perfa . . ." She shook her head in frustration.

"Perfidy?" he suggested.

"Oui. Perfidy. Exactly, yes. Do you know what this document shows?"

"Don't reckon that I do, no."

"During your war, when the puppet emperor Maximillian ruled Mexico, these people who are no true Frenchmen, they made common cause with your enemy, the . . . what did they call themselves again?"

"The Confederacy," Longarm said. "Confederate States of America."

"Oui, of course. Confederacy. France would have made cause with them, do you see."

"That's no secret," Longarm told her. "France supplied a lot of guns and powder and such to the Rebs. So did England, for that matter."

"Yes, but what your government it does not know is that France was prepared then to send troops to assist them. Then when the war was won by these Confederacies, they would cede the land of the Louisiana Purchase back to France. Much of these land, not all. The Confederacies, they would keep Louisiana and Texas. All the land to the west would be returned to France, to be ruled from Mexico. They would have invaded your country, m'sieur.

"And they are desperate that this not be known by your government because even today there are those in France who would seek to reclaim these land. By force if need be. So you see now important it is that you help me . . . that you help us . . . to expose these madmen before they start a war between your country and mine.

"You must not longer assist this traitorous marquis. He would restore the monarchy, and in his delusion he . . . they . . . would seek to conquer this North America. They tried this until they were stopped by Juarez, m'sieur. If they have the chance, they will try again. But you can stop them, m'sieur. Help us to find the document. Help us to save your country from the madmen. And my country too, yes?" She kissed him, and her hand crept to his crotch, her fingers curling tight and warm around his limp—only temporarily limp, that is—pecker.

"Help me," she whispered.

Longarm ignored the plea and rolled Genevieve onto her back. He inserted his knee between her thighs and levered her legs apart, then entered her.

Genevieve gasped and began to make small whimpering, mewling noises as he stroked steadily in and out.

He was enjoying himself. No doubt about that. But he did have to admit to a certain amount of distraction.

Twice during the girl's explanations he had heard soil crunch underfoot as someone immediately outside the hay shed fidgeted.

Not that Longarm minded the sonuvabitch being out there. It was a convenience really. Kept any other hotel occupant from blundering in and disturbing this tender little drama Genevieve and Mansard were playing out.

He just wished to hell he had some way to know if any small part of what she said was true.

"Oh, Custis. *Mon cher*," Genevieve cried out. "Yes. Yes. Yes." Her fingernails raked his back and her slim hips pumped furiously beneath him, battering his belly with hers. Longarm took his cue from her and speeded the pace of his thrusting.

Yep. He sure did wish he knew what was true here.

Chapter 32

"So where would the..." He lowered his voice and looked carefully around to make sure no one else was interested in the conversation. "Where is this gold s'posed to be, Jean-Claude?"

"Tomorrow," the Frenchman said. "We will go tomorrow to see if the"—he too looked surreptitiously around the room full of snoring travelers—"if the material is there."

"You know where to look?"

Jean-Claude hesitated. "Perhaps. With your help."

Whatever the hell that meant, Longarm thought. The man knew or he did not know. What could be so complicated about that? "Tomorrow then," Longarm said.

Longarm kicked his boots off—he did not trust the place far enough to strip out of his clothes, putting his faith in neither the other patrons nor the suspect cleanliness of the blankets—but he drew the line at sleeping with his boots on. Besides, the proprietor claimed that habit got the blankets muddy, and heaven forbid there should be a taint of soil on the bedding. Which smelled of whiskey and tobacco and half-a-dozen other odors Longarm decided he would rather not try to identify. He suspected this was one of those times when a man is better off not knowing quite all the truth.

"G'night, Jean-Claude."

The Frenchman did not answer. Longarm did not bother rolling over to see if Gilbert was being snobbish again or if he'd simply fallen asleep already.

He did not find it possible to drop immediately into sleep himself, however. Longarm lay awake for a considerable time thinking about the evening.

It was obvious that Louis Mansard was changing his tactics. For now.

His first inclination was straightforward and blunt. Kill the bodyguard and kidnap the marquis. After all, Jean-Claude held the key in the document that had come into the possession of the French government. Capture Jean-Claude, take the document from him, and have every bit as much knowledge as did the government. Simple.

But simple no longer. Once Jean-Claude burned the document, Mansard had only Jean-Claude's memory to guide him. He needed Jean-Claude and needed him both alive and cooperative. Exactly how he intended to arrange the latter part remained unknown.

Now, though, instead of trying to kill Longarm to get him out of the way, they wanted to recruit him.

Why? Did Mansard think Jean-Claude had already told Longarm where the secrets were buried and that Longarm, not being French and feeling no attachment to the government of France, would be willing to disclose that information?

Genevieve had not tried to turn his loyalties. So far. Longarm suspected Mansard had sent her tonight to seduce him, probably believing he would become so besotted by the girl that he would be willing to help her find . . . what?

That in itself was a weighty unknown. Just what the hell were they looking for here? Gold was the declared object of the search, but Longarm hadn't believed that from the earliest moments of the expedition. There just was not that much gold missing. Not from the perspective of a sovereign nation's treasury. One or two or three chests of gold coins would hardly be worth the attention of the French nation. Not at this level of pursuit. And not in secret.

Had they only wanted their gold back—assuming there really was any gold—France could simply have asked the United States for permission to go fetch it home. That approval would have been easily come by.

So why in the world did they involve one lone deputy U.S. marshal? And why send Jean-Claude on his own? And why pursue the effort by way of Denver and not New Orleans or Austin? Either of those would be more logical than appealing to Billy Vail all the way up in Denver.

Secrecy was the answer Longarm got to that one once he got to thinking about it. The ambassador and Jean-Claude wanted this done in secrecy.

Did that mean it did not have the full approval of their own government then? Could Mansard really be representing official French interests here?

For damn sure Jean-Claude had not told Longarm the truth. Hell, Longarm had known that from the first moments, and the fact was all the clearer now.

But how far could he trust the few things Genevieve reported to him this evening?

Not very damn far. Not only would the girl cheerfully lie—which pretty much every woman does anyway—but she herself might not have been told the truth.

Mansard . . . a thought occurred to Longarm. Mansard was obviously the man in charge of the opposition, and he had little help to back him up now. Longarm had succeeded in killing the assassins on the riverboat and another outside the whorehouse that night, then the one at the wagon when he rescued Jean-Claude from them. It could be that Mansard was running out of trusted hired hands and so was forced to change his tactics. If you can't beat 'em, hire 'em.

That was a distinct possibility. They could really hope to recruit Longarm to their cause.

Longarm had been careful to give Mansard hope about that this evening. Before he buttoned his britches and came back inside the hotel, he had assured Genevieve du Charme he would consider the things she said. He knew good and well she would immediately report that promise to Louis Mansard.

Longarm figured the delaying tactic should give Jean-Claude time to find whatever it was he wanted . . . the document that Genevieve claimed or gold or whatever . . . while Mansard bided his time.

It was puzzling, Longarm thought. And Genevieve had made him tired. The hell with all this thinking. He closed his eyes and let himself sink into a light and wary sleep.

"D'you see what you're looking for?" Longarm asked. It was mid-morning and he and Jean-Claude Gilbert had been walking the streets of Gros Teton since breakfast. Jean-Claude concentrated his attention on the scenery— or what passed for scenery in this dreary and sunbaked little community—while Longarm kept a wary eye out for Mansard or his remaining gunman. So far he had seen neither, although at one point he did think he caught a glimpse of Genevieve inside the window of a seamstress's shop.

"Non," Jean-Claude said curtly.

"Think it might help any if I was t' know what you're looking for?"

"Perhaps, m'sieur, but I was hoping to understand the message myself."

"You got a message?" Longarm asked.

"Not recent, no. I mean the writing that was left behind,

the message that I commit to memory before burning."

"Do whatever you want, Jean-Claude, but I can't help you look if I got no idea what we're looking for."

"Yes, but . . . give me time, eh?"

Longarm shrugged and reached for a brandy crook. If he didn't soon find a source of good-quality cheroots, he might actually come to like these sticky-sweet-flavored little crooks. And wouldn't that be a pisser.

"Let me know," Longarm said, his eyes constantly sweeping the surrounding area for Mansard or his henchman.

Chapter 33

"Dammit, Jean-Claude, it's time," Longarm declared. It was late afternoon, and he was about fed up with the Frenchman's mindless wanderings. Up and down the length and breadth of every street and alley in town. They'd even crept around the backs of every shed, barn, or outhouse they could find. Longarm's feet were sore, he was tired, he wanted supper and a drink, and his patience was plumb used up.

"This is getting on t' the point of bein' ridiculous," he grumbled.

Jean-Claude shook his head sadly and said, "*Oui.* So it must be."

"Are you finally gonna tell me what it is that you been looking for so serious all day?"

"*Oui.*"

They were standing on a street corner not far from the hotel. Longarm glanced around to guard against any immediate threat, but he no longer expected one. Not at this point.

After all, he'd spotted Genevieve at least three times during the course of the day, and Mansard's tame gun-

157

hand on several other occasions. Always at a distance. Always watching, but only watching.

If any of them intended any mischief, they'd had more than enough opportunity for it while Jean-Claude was busy inspecting the trash bins and garbage piles of Gros Teton . . . or whatever the hell it was he'd been doing all day.

One thing Longarm noticed was that he had *not* noticed Louis Mansard. Mansard seemed to have disappeared. They surely must have passed by his windows, wherever he was keeping himself, but the man remained well out of sight if not out of mind.

Tonight, Longarm thought. Perhaps Mansard would show himself tonight. Genevieve said Longarm could have today to think over the things she'd told him last night. Tonight she expected an answer. Would Longarm help them? Or not?

Longarm suspected he would be presented with clear choices tonight, the second of which might or might not be openly stated. He could continue to enjoy the pleasures of Genevieve du Charme's supple and lovely body . . . or he would have to be eliminated. Regrettably, of course.

But that he would worry about later. Right now, he just wanted a meal and a drink and to get the hell off his feet.

"Well?" he prompted.

Jean-Claude grimaced. "You will think I am foolish, m'sieur."

"Mister, I already think you're foolish."

The Marquis de Sant Cerre's nostrils flared, and he drew himself stiffly to his full height. He was not accustomed to be addressed so rudely. He looked ready to explode. But only for a moment. More than likely, he too was footsore and hungry, and by now probably was discouraged as well.

"X marks the spot," he said in a soft voice.

"Par'n me?"

"I said 'X marks the spot,' " Jean-Claude repeated.

"Oh, I heard you all right. But what the fuck is that s'posed t' mean?"

"I . . . I do not know. It is what was written."

"Good God, Jean-Claude!" Longarm snorted. "X marks the spot. Don't you know that's the fake locator in every buried-treasure hoax there's ever been? X marks the fucking spot indeed. Just how gullible is your government anyway to send you on a wild-goose chase over some son of a bitch's imagination."

"I know, I know," Jean-Claude said, wringing his hands and looking quite thoroughly embarrassed. "But this document . . . it is real. It is no hoax, m'sieur. I would . . . what am I saying? I have staked my life on this. And yours. We are both in jeopardy, m'sieur, because 'X marks the spot.' But . . . where is this X, eh? I ask you that. Where am I to find the X that marks the spot we seek?"

"New Mexico maybe?" Longarm suggested. "Or Colorado."

"M'sieur, I have a confession to make. It is neither of those. It is here. In Gros Teton in your province . . . excuse me, your state . . . of Texas. Of this I am certain."

"The document specified Texas?"

Jean-Claude nodded.

"Then why . . . oh, hell. Never mind. You was just throwing some misdirection around."

"Oui. So I was, m'sieur. But we are here now. There is no X that I can see."

"So you didn't actually need me t' help search. Fine. Why did you drag me along then?"

"I hoped . . . we hoped . . . that the presence of a representative of the American government . . ." He spread his hands and looked downright sheepish.

"You thought Mansard and his outfit wouldn't want t'

159

insult the U.S. gummint and get into a international scrape by messing with a U.S. deputy, is that it?"

Jean-Claude nodded. "We were wrong, of course. For this I apologize. We have put you in danger to no avail. I am sorry."

"Jean-Claude, I didn't know you was capable of utterin' those words. Truth to tell, I like you better for hearing it."

Gilbert gave him a searching, speculative look, but said nothing.

Longarm saw Mansard's gunman loafing outside a harness maker's shop at the end of the next block. He resisted an impulse to wave and call out a howdy. "Tell you what, Jean-Claude. Let's go have us something to eat, and afterward I'll set us up to a drink or two before I go out an' tend to the horses. How does that sound?"

"Oui, m'sieur. Merci."

"Mercy? That's in short supply out here in Texas, Jean-Claude." He smiled. "But we got plenty of whiskey."

"No, no, I meant. . . ."

"I know what you meant, Jean-Claude. I was just funnin' you."

"Oh. I see."

"C'mon. We'll try that café a couple blocks over. I been smelling the cooking there most all day long, and at this point I'm so hungry that damn if it isn't commencing to smell good to me."

Longarm smiled, and led the way toward the greasy little café they must have walked past two dozen times during the course of the day.

But . . . Lordy!

X marks the spot.

Indeed.

160

Chapter 34

Longarm fiddled around after supper until it was nearly dark before he went out to catch the horses out of the pen and lead them over to the hotel's hay shed. The beasts took their time about eating, yet there was no sign of Genevieve by the time he returned the horses and turned them loose in the public corral.

Longarm felt a hint of alarm at the possibility he was being set up for another murder try, and was walking on eggshells by the time he got back to the shed.

"Custis, my big beautiful boy." Her voice came to him out of the darkness deep inside the hay shed.

"Where the hell are you?"

He heard her giggle. "I have been here the whole time, *mon cher*. You are very good to watch. So strong. So handsome."

Compliments aside, it spooked the hell out of him to realize she'd been there and he hadn't had any hint of it.

Still, if he wanted proof that Mansard did not intend to kill him—yet—that would serve to do the job.

"Where are you? I can't see you?" Which was not entirely true. His eyes were quickly adjusting to the gloom at the back of the shed, and he could make out movement and a shape, very slightly pale against a backdrop of complete and utter blackness, behind the pile of soft hay.

"Here," she whispered. "I am naked for you. That is why I could not allow myself to be seen, my sweet. Anyone could walk in, and I am here only for you. Now come to me. Quickly. I cannot wait any the longer."

He joined her, and Genevieve pressed herself tight against him, her arms wrapped around his neck and her mouth eagerly searching his. Her breath mixed with his, and her tongue probed inside his mouth.

She hadn't been lying. The pretty French girl was naked. And in a hurry.

Her fingers fumbled his clothing open, and she dropped to her knees to take him briefly into the wet heat of her mouth while she unfastened his gunbelt and tossed it aside.

His erection was hard enough to fuck a knothole . . . before the plug was knocked out of it.

She cupped his balls in her hands, her fingernails lightly teasing that exquisitely sensitive patch of flesh between his balls and his asshole, and she licked and sucked her way up his belly and onto his nipples.

"Take me. Please. Please. Take me."

Genevieve tugged him down on top of her in the hay. Her legs opened to him, and she gasped when he rammed his cock into her slender body.

"Yes, yes, please." She bit his earlobe. Probably drew blood. Longarm retaliated by beating her with the flat of his belly.

Genevieve cried out. She reached beneath the clothing on his upper body and raked his back with her nails.

The girl was like a cat in heat, hot and frantic and wildly bucking.

He felt her spasms of completion twice before he came, and a third time that was simultaneous with his own massive explosion.

"Lordy," he mumbled as he rolled off her.

"Ah, ma sweet." She laughed and told him something long and complicated in French. That was all right. He was too thoroughly spent to make sense of it even if she'd said it in English, he was sure.

"That," he said, gulping for breath, "was almighty good."

"*Oui*, so it was, *non*?" She sounded pleased. Well, so was he. Much more pleased and he reckoned he'd pass clean out.

"Pity we're laying in all this hay, though," he said. "After something that good, I could do with a smoke. But I reckon that'll have to wait."

"Yes." She giggled. "But I was so hot I feared we would start the fire from the heat of our bodies."

"I've heard that sort o' thing can happen," Longarm said in mock seriousness.

"*Oui?*"

"Yeah. We." He laughed. Funny thing, but he wasn't feeling so tired now like he had been after the day of searching for a non-existent X.

Or anyway, the tiredness he felt now was of a different and much more enjoyable sort.

"My sweet," Genevieve said in a lower but more businesslike tone.

Now comes the time to pay her back, Longarm thought. He was right.

"You have thought about what we discussed last night?"

"Sure," Longarm told her.

"You realize that what we try to do is in the best interests of your own country? These people the marquis supports, they would revive those plans of old. They would take all of Mexico for their own. They might even start the war with your country, do you see. They still want to reclaim the land from the Louisiana Purchase.

163

Maybe even Louisiana and Texas now that there is no Confederate States to sign treaties with. You must help us, *mon cher*. You must prevent the war between your nation and mine. You must tell us where the documents are hidden."

Longarm kissed her. "What I got t' do, pretty girl, is what my boss an' the government of these here United States ordered me t' do. What I got to do, Jenny girl, is help Jean-Claude an' keep him safe from the likes o' you and Louis Mansard. Even if that means you won't fuck me no more."

Genevieve scowled and jerked back away from him.

She shouted something in French and threw herself to the side.

She landed, he couldn't help but notice, exactly where she'd dropped his Colt and gunbelt a quarter hour or so earlier.

Longarm bounced to his feet.

He stood at the back of the shed with his trousers down around his ankles, his coat and vest and shirt flopping open . . . and his .44 somewhere underneath a screaming, spitting, cursing Genevieve du Charme.

A third form materialized at the open front of the shed. A man's shape. With a pistol in his hand and a wide-brimmed hat that identified him as Louis Mansard's hired killer.

"Oh, shit," Longarm barked to no one in particular.

Chapter 35

The gunhand held his revolver leveled, and Genevieve stopped her cussing and carrying on. Longarm stood still as a statue while Louis Mansard stepped into the shed-front opening.

"We meet at last, m'sieur," the leader of the gang of Frenchies said.

Genevieve sat up and began brushing hay stems out of her hair. She tidied up first, then got around to finding her clothing and starting to get dressed. Longarm gathered she'd been naked in front of menfolk before this particular moment.

"You've gone to a lot of trouble here," Longarm said.

Mansard shrugged. "It is nothing if you will help us."

"I already told the young ... uh ... lady what my answer has t' be."

"But that is such a terrible pity, m'sieur. You are in the employ of your country. You do them a disservice if you allow the royalists to win. You see, m'sieur, with that document my party can bring them down. Their ambitions of empire will be ended for all time. And your wonderful country, m'sieur, will be safe from incursion."

"You're a fine-speakin' man, Mr. Mansard. I daresay

you'd do well in politics in most any country, this one included. But those fine sentiments don't go real well with what I've seen from you. Kidnap. Attempted murder. Hired assassins." Longarm nodded toward the fellow standing beside Mansard. The one with the rather large revolver in his hand. "Like that one. And the others that didn't make it this far. For a man who's singing the praises of the U.S. of A., you don't much seem t' mind breakin' our laws."

"An error in judgment," Mansard said calmly. "A result of our . . ." He paused and said something in French to the gunman.

"Zeal," the man with the Colt said.

"Ah, yes. Zeal. A result of our zeal as we attempt to save our country and yours at the same time, m'sieur. We must have that document. We must."

"An' if I feel obligated to oppose that effort?" Longarm asked.

"Regrettably, m'sieur, I cannot permit myself to fail. I too am, as you say, obligated. I must insist on your co-operation. At the very least . . . and believe me, m'sieur, I appreciate a man's honor . . . I do not expect you to actively participate in our, shall we say, encouragement that the marquis share with us his knowledge. But at the very least, you must agree to stand aside and cease your interference."

Longarm smiled. "Yeah, I can see how you'd want me t' back off. Seeing as how you're running out o' troops under your command. Just that cheap gunman there an' the slut." He nodded toward Genevieve.

She, hearing the insult, flew into a rage. She leaped at Longarm, spitting and scratching, all tooth, claw, and toe-nail as she came at him.

Longarm accepted the onslaught.

And sidled half a step to the side so Genevieve was between him and the gunman.

"Shoot, Pierre, shoot!" Mansard screamed when he saw what Longarm was doing. "Never mind her. Shoot. Shoot!"

Pierre was slow to heed the instructions.

And why not? After all, he knew Longarm's Colt to be buried in the hay two long paces distant. Even if Longarm knew precisely where the gun had fallen, there was no way he could get to it before Pierre could pump half a cylinder of .45's into him.

Longarm, however, had no intention of going for his own revolver.

Instead, he held Genevieve off with an extended left arm while his right hand dipped into his vest pocket and brought out the little brass-framed derringer he always carried there.

In the darkness of the shed, Pierre could not see the danger, and continued to hesitate while Mansard continued to bluster and screech for the man to shoot, quickly, shoot.

"Let it go, Pierre," Longarm warned. "You're under arrest for . . . hell, I dunno . . . assault on a federal officer. Attempted murder too. Now drop the damn gun and give yourself up."

Pierre finally decided to heed his boss's instructions. He cocked his revolver—silly sonuvabitch had been waving it around with the hammer down, which Longarm considered to be a truly stupid thing—and tried to take aim, his hand shifting back and forth as Genevieve snarled and jerked about in front of Longarm.

"Drop it, Pierre. No more warnings."

Pierre did not drop it.

Longarm's stubby little .44 derringer roared, the tiny barrel exaggerating both the sound of the explosion and the resulting fireball. The muzzle flash illuminated the inside of the shed as completely as a photographer's flash powder could have done, and as briefly.

Longarm blinked, trying to regain night vision after the burst of bright light.

When he could see again, Louis Mansard was not to be found.

But Pierre was. The failed assassin lay curled on the ground at the mouth of the shed, clutching his belly with both hands, his Colt forgotten on the ground beside him.

Genevieve continued to shriek and scratch.

"I'm getting tired of this," Longarm snapped. "Now calm down."

"Bastard. Son of beech." She continued hurling imprecations, mostly in French, but with an occasional insult in English as well.

"Stop it," Longarm said as he leaned back to avoid her raking, clawing fingernails. "D'you hear me? Stop it."

She tried to kick him in the nuts, and he was barely able to avoid the blow, hampered as he was by still having his trousers around his ankles.

"I warned you," he said.

He pocketed the derringer and delivered a short, chopping right hand onto the shelf of Genevieve du Charme's pretty jaw.

She was not going to like that. But then he had already begun to suspect that she did not really and truly love him anyway.

She went out like a candle in a windstorm. Her eyes rolled back in her head and she collapsed, out cold.

Even so, Longarm knew better than to trust her. He let her fall—hell, the hay was soft enough—and kicked around for a moment to find and recover his gunbelt, then walked rather warily to the front of the shed.

He kicked Pierre's gun out of the man's reach. Not that Pierre was in any condition to care about the Colt, but the man who takes unnecessary chances can find himself quite unnecessarily dead.

Then he looked around for Mansard.

168

That worthy gentleman had scarpered.

Longarm knelt down and checked on Pierre. The man was gutshot and in agony. He was dying. If he was lucky, he would get it over with quickly. With a wound like that, to live would be a curse. He would spend whatever time he had left screaming for the pain to cease, but it would not. Not until the final breath left him and a welcome death gave him relief.

Longarm made sure Pierre had no more weapons. He shoved the man's Colt into his own waistband and went to check on Genevieve, who was beginning to regain consciousness.

"Welcome back," Longarm said once he was sure she was aware of her surroundings.

"What . . . aiyee!" She began screeching and ranting all over again.

But not scratching, hitting, or clawing. Not this time. Longarm had her wrists clamped tight in steel handcuffs locked behind her back.

She tried to kick him, but slipped in the loose hay and ended up sprawling on her pretty ass.

"You just don't know how much I enjoyed putting those bracelets on you, honey," he told her.

She made some suggestions, again mostly in French. The few he was able to understand he would not have been able to perform even had he wanted to.

"If you're ready, honey, we'll go hunt up a jail to put you in. An' maybe let the doctor know your friend here needs some laudanum to take the edge off his pain while he's waitin' to die."

Longarm took a firm grip on Genevieve's handcuffs and hauled her bodily upright. Still holding onto her, he walked her out into the alley and onto the street, wondering what they had in this town by way of a jail and who he should see to get her into it.

Chapter 36

"Then it is over," Jean-Claude said at breakfast the next morning. "Louis has run away. His people are either dead or in custody. Now all we need is for you to find the X that marks the spot, eh?"

"Sure. We'll go out an' look for an X again. What d'you figure? It'll be painted on the ground? Carved in a tree trunk? No, I reckon that wouldn't be real likely. It's prob'ly, what, thirty miles to the next tree?" Longarm became serious. "Jean-Claude, don't let your guard down yet. Pierre is dying and Genevieve is behind bars, but we don't know where Louis is. He's still a threat."

"No, m'sieur. I assure you. I know this man. He has not the . . . how would you Americans say it . . . he has not the balls to face either one of us without his thugs and his spies. Alone, Louis is a bee with no stinger. A snake without venom. No, m'sieur, now we only need to find our X."

Longarm smiled a little. "You're an optimist, Jean-Claude. In order for the writer of those directions to talk about an X, there must've been a map included."

"There was no map."

"Not when you got the stuff," Longarm said. "That

doesn't mean there never was a map. There pretty much has to've been one. With the X marked on it. Without that . . ." He shrugged. "It's like having a key but not having any notion where the lock is that your key fits. You know the stuff was buried . . . no, I shouldn't say buried, should I . . . it was hidden someplace around Gros Teton, Texas. Jean-Claude, step outside, why don't you, and take a good, long look around you. There's nothing but salt flat and scrub desert for a hundred damn miles in any direction you want to go."

Jean-Claude sighed. And looked with suspicion at the gray and tasteless bowl of grits in front of him. "This country, m'sieur, it is not civilized."

Longarm laughed. "That's true even by our standards. What d'you say we go back to New Orleans. I'll escort you that far, then leave you there with the French consul. I think you'll be safe enough once it's plain the search is over, but I'll see you that far, then head back to Denver."

"Yes," Jean-Claude said stubbornly. "We will do this. Just as soon as we have found the, um, the material."

"If you don't want those grits, Jean-Claude, give them to me."

Gilbert made a sour face and pushed the dish across the table.

Later, after coffee and a brandy crook, Longarm stretched and said, "I want to go check on Pierre, see if he's kicked the bucket yet. For his sake, I kinda hope he has. And I wanta stop by and see if my prisoner is all right. I want to make sure no local constable takes it on himself to accept a piece of ass in lieu of bail."

"Fine. I will go back to the hotel and wait for you."

"Jean-Claude, if it's all the same to you, I'd like for you to go with me. We got no idea where Mansard is, and I don't want him making one last kidnap attempt when my back is turned."

"I assure you, m'sieur, that alone Louis is toothless."

"Has it occurred to you, Jean-Claude, that Mansard may not be alone anymore? If he has money, he might try to hire himself some local gunslicks to help him finish the job."

"I did not think. . . ."

"Come with me. Please."

"Very well. If you wish it."

"I do."

They stopped first at the doctor's office. The Gros Teton doc was a shriveled little wisp of a man who reminded Longarm of a raisin, something once plump and healthy that had become dried out and withered in the burning desert sun. Even so, the man kept a tidy office and seemed to know what he was doing.

He greeted Longarm with a nod, but no particular enthusiasm. "You would do us all a favor if you would learn to shoot straighter," he said. "Your victim lives. It would have been better if you killed him outright."

Last night Longarm had not bothered to explain the circumstances of his encounter with Pierre. He did so now. The doctor did not seem to give a particular damn. "I do not like to see suffering, Marshal. That's why I became a physician to begin with." He snorted. "Do you know what I really wanted to be? A veterinarian, that's what. But I am too softhearted to see animals suffer and then sometimes have to put them out of their misery. I cannot do it. And so I became a doctor. So I can stand by helpless while a young and otherwise healthy man dies a slow death from a bullet wound that has turned his intestines into goulash."

"I would've preferred something else my own self, doctor, but he wouldn't drop the gun he was fixing to shoot me with. If you want regrets, find out who his folks were and get them there. I got none to offer."

"Leave me, would you, please? Please?"

"I'd like to talk to him first. Maybe he can tell me something about his boss or what they planned to do."

"I am sorry." The doctor did not sound sorry in the

least. If anything, he sounded pleased that he was able to thwart Longarm's request. "That will not be possible. You can hear for yourself that he is not screaming now. The pain is not yet bad enough to overcome the opiates I have given him. Tomorrow, two days from now for sure, there will be nothing I can do to ease his suffering. The pain will surpass my puny efforts, and he will suffer. He will suffer horribly. Unless I help him out of this life and into the next, and that is something I am sworn not to do.

"I tell you, Marshal, there are times when I hate the fate that made me a physician. This is one of those times. Now leave, please. He is unconscious. By the time pain drags him awake again, he will care nothing about questions. You will never be able to talk with him. Now go. Please go."

Longarm went. But he did not apologize. Better Pierre lie there with a bullet in his guts, Longarm figured, than for *him* to be the one who was shot and dying.

Fuck Pierre. Fuck the doctor, too.

But he would not be fucking Genevieve, he thought as he made his way to the rock-walled jail set behind the town hall. During their daylong search yesterday, he had noticed the tiny stone building but mistook it for a two-holer outhouse. The damn thing was that small.

He was pleased to see the padlock still held the iron-reinforced door shut.

"Mornin' there, Genevieve," he said to the single barred window set high under the eaves of the roof.

Her response was a torrent of French. Which Jean-Claude responded to in kind. The two of them yammered back and forth through the window for several minutes before Gilbert said, "She tells me you betrayed her."

"I did?"

"*Oui.* She says you made her fall in love with you, then you took her virginity, and when you were done, you discarded her like a rag you used to wipe yourself. She is very angry with you, m'sieur."

Longarm chuckled. "Jean-Claude, if you believe that, then you'd believe in a bullshit buried-treasure hunt where an X marks the spot."

"You are mocking me again."

"Yeah, I guess I am. Sorry."

The two Frenchies jawed back and forth for a little longer.

"Ask her where Mansard was holed up yesterday," Longarm suggested.

After more conversation, Gilbert said, "She tell me she would make me very happy if I arrange to have her freed from here. She says she would make us both very happy."

"She could do that if she took a mind to," Longarm confirmed. "She can make a man's toes curl, an' that's a fact."

"She is only a girl," Jean-Claude said. "She claims she herself has never tried to hurt you. Has never tried to hurt anyone. She only used her charms to entice and to please. Is this true?"

"Oh, I reckon you could say that it is. What about when they was holding you captive? Did she seem dangerous to you?"

"She seemed a beautiful young woman. Misguided but harmless."

"You're telling me you want to let her out?" Longarm asked.

"If she will tell us where we can find Louis, yes, I think so."

"All right. If she will tell us . . ."

"In a room at the rear of the barber's," Genevieve called out from inside the jail. "He paid the man for secrecy. Twenty dollars in cash and twenty minutes of my time. Ask the barber. He will tell you."

"We'll be right back, honey, to see about gettin' you sprung," Longarm tossed over his shoulder as he dragged Jean-Claude off toward the barbershop.

Chapter 37

"Sure, he was here. French fella. He never gave me a name and I never asked him for one. But he paid me twenty dollars hard money for the room and to keep my mouth shut. Which I will admit that I done, just like he asked. I probably wouldn't tell you about him now if he was still staying here. Wouldn't be right to take his money and then blab when he said I shouldn't. But he's gone now, so I don't see as it matters anymore."

"He's gone, you say?"

"I do say. Came rushing in here last night. By himself, he was. Grabbed up his things and headed back out the door. I haven't seen him since."

"Mind if I take a look?" Longarm asked.

"Help yourself." The barber pointed toward a door in the back wall.

Longarm drew his Colt before he shoved the door open and went in fast and at an angle. Just in case the barber was lying.

The caution was wasted . . . although better to be overly cautious a hundred times for no reason than to forget just once when there was danger on the other side of the door.

The room was empty save for a mattress ticking laid

out on the floor, a basin and pitcher, and five leather traveling cases. Those would belong to Genevieve, Longarm assumed, and perhaps to Pierre as well.

But there was no sign of Louis Mansard.

Longarm pushed the Colt back into his holster and returned to the barbershop, where Jean-Claude was waiting. "He was here, I reckon, but not now."

"I told you that," the barber said.

"So you did."

"I'm not giving back the twenty dollars. He offered it. I didn't extort him or nothing."

"No, sir, the money is yours. You didn't do anything wrong." Longarm grinned. "Anyway, there wouldn't be any way you could return all of what you were paid."

"I don't know what you're talking about," the barber protested. The blush that burned his earlobes suggested he was not being entirely truthful about that. But hell, Longarm couldn't blame him for poking a pretty girl. Not unless the barber was a married man, and even if he was, that was on his own conscience, not Longarm's.

"Thanks for your help," Longarm told him.

"What about those other bags?"

"The lady will be back for them. When she's taken whatever is hers, you might give the younger man's stuff to the doctor across the street over there. There might be something in them worth accepting as his pay for tending the fellow."

"He's the one that was shot last night?"

"That's right."

The barber shuddered. "I don't like violence."

"Neither do I," Longarm told him.

"I told you Louis would run away," Jean-Claude said once they were back on the street.

"Yes, I expect you did at that."

"Shall we go find the sheriff now and see about having Miss du Charme released? It was a promise, no?"

"It was a promise, yes."

They returned to the town hall and went inside. The town constable was a man named Jennings. Last night he had not been happy about the idea of putting a woman in jail. It offended his sense of propriety to force a lady to use a bucket for her private needs, or so he said.

"Put in a tub and hot water if you please," Longarm had told him at the time. "Just be damn sure she isn't let out. Not for any reason. Not even if she says she has to pee-pee. Understand? For no reason at all, or I'll put you in your own jail, and don't for a minute think I'm not capable of doing it."

Jennings seemed delighted now to hear that Longarm wanted the prisoner released.

"Yes. Wonderful. Wait right here. I'll go get the key."

The constable's "office" was a desk set in a corner of the town clerk's office. There was a counter where citizens could come to transact their business, and several racks of the hugely heavy canvas-covered ledgers without which no government could possibly function.

Jennings disappeared into another room, and Longarm and Jean-Claude occupied themselves by admiring a handful of drawings on the walls.

Actually, it was Gilbert who was paying attention to them. He pointed them out to Longarm, and offered some rather biting criticism of the artist's efforts.

As far as Longarm was concerned, anybody who could draw something good enough that you could figure out what it was supposed to be, that fellow was head and shoulders above anything Longarm would be able to do, so he wasn't in much of a position to grumble about the other fellow's work.

"No, you can see. Here. And here. The perspective is wrong. And look. He makes the town appear larger than it is. Makes that sad little tumbledown church look like a cathedral. See? He exaggerates shamelessly."

"It's art, Jean-Claude. Art doesn't have to be exactly truthful, does it?"

"This? Bah! This is not art. This is not even talented sketching. No, m'sieur. Look here."

Longarm had no desire to look there. And anyway, Jennings was back. He had the key and he was smiling.

"C'mon, Jean-Claude. Let's spring your girlfriend. Then we can go collect that hidden stuff you're after."

"M'sieur? Pardon?"

Longarm grinned at him. "It's all right. I know what spot your X is marking."

Chapter 38

There was no sign of it now. Over the years it must have rotted away, or some unbelieving soul who wanted an easy source of firewood had burned it. Longarm guessed the latter since the time span was not all that great, but for whatever reason, the cross that once had been on the peak of the taller of Gros Teton's two rocky tits was gone now. There was no sign of it, else they might have figured out the X thing before.

It was not, Longarm reasoned now, an X at all but a cross. And those drawings in the town clerk's office clearly showed a rather short cross—short due to the lack of available wood perhaps?—erected atop the mound that was closer to the town.

"But of course," Jean-Claude said with enthusiasm. "It must be so."

The two of them let Constable Jennings take charge of releasing Genevieve while they went directly to the foot of the rocky outcrop.

Longarm knew nothing about geology. All he knew of for sure about these miniature hills, neither of which was particularly large, was that they consisted of a dark and gritty stone that was cracked and broken and shaped like inverted cones, that simple fact leading to their designation as tit shapes. Longarm still thought it would take an awfully horny man to make that connection.

"Hurry, m'sieur," Jean-Claude kept urging him as he almost ran up the steep slope.

The damn Frenchman was in awfully good shape, Longarm thought as he labored to keep up, scrambling for handholds as well as solid footing on his way toward the top.

Longarm was still a good ten feet from the summit when he heard Jean-Claude roar with excitement.

"This must be it, m'sieur. Look here."

Longarm puffed the rest of the way upward to join Gilbert, who was on hands and knees now.

Longarm could see why. Very near to the topmost point on the mound, there was a depression gouged into solid rock and filled in now with shards and stone chips. On the back side of the hill, he could see the weathered, hand-hewn planks that must once have been the cross. The cross looked like it had fallen apart years ago and no one had bothered to repair or replace it here.

It was not inconceivable, Longarm thought, that the cross could have been planted originally by the early Spaniards. After all, the salt flat that drew men here would have existed for hundreds, probably thousands of years. And the Spanish friars who first came to this country were known for planting the cross wherever they went. They were also known for their extreme cruelty to the natives. But that was a different matter entirely, and it could well have been they who made regular trips to the salt supply and placed the cross above this chosen site to guide and protect them.

Whoever it was, and however long ago, it had taken considerable effort to dig a socket in the stone to hold the base of the cross.

The bottom of what must have been the upright member was splintered and broken. Further down the slope from it, Longarm spotted a matching chunk that was about two or two and a half feet long and showed much less decay. That, he figured, would have been the part of the upright that was set into the socket.

And while the cross itself may have weathered and fallen from natural causes—indeed very likely did so—it took deliberate effort to dig out the base and toss it down the slope.

He looked again at the socket, and saw rock chips filling it to the rim. Those chips hadn't gotten there on their own, he realized. Where the hell could they have fallen from? They were already at the top of the mound, and gravel just doesn't drop out of the sky. Somebody placed those into the hole.

And something else as well?

They would find out very soon, for Jean-Claude was already clawing the egg-sized stones out of the hole and shoving them aside.

The marquis was sure to ruin his nails, Longarm mused. Hell, he hadn't known Jean-Claude was capable of manual labor like this.

As it turned out, he did not have to dig very long.

"I found something," Jean-Claude yelped. He cleared away a few final stones, and reached down with both hands to grasp and extract a leather-wrapped bundle. From the way he handled it, Longarm knew it was not gold he was pulling out of that hole.

The rotted leather fell apart in Jean-Claude's hands, exposing a book—it appeared to be a small ledger or journal, perhaps a diary—and another, smaller bundle wrapped in oilcloth.

Jean-Claude opened that. It contained a document, several very large pages secured together with ribbon and carrying an ornate wax seal at the bottom of the first page.

"Is that what you been looking for, Jean-Claude?"

Gilbert did not answer.

"Mansard told me that paper has something t' do with French plans to take the Louisiana Purchase back from the United States, Jean-Claude. Was he telling me the truth? Is that some sort of instruction to Maximillian to prepare the way for it? Is that what your government was afraid for anybody to find an' use against them? Is that it, Jean-Claude? Tell me, dammit!"

"Do you want to read it for yourself, Long?" Gilbert thrust the papers at Longarm.

"You know better. You know I can't read French."

Gilbert shrugged. "That is not my fault, m'sieur. I am open with you. I offer for you to inspect this if you wish. You do not wish. So be it."

"I think what we better do here is that I'll take that there paper, Jean-Claude. For safekeeping, y'see. After all, that's what I'm here for. I'll keep it safe for you, an' after the two of us gets to Washington with it, then I'll turn it over to you."

"This is not acceptable, m'sieur. This document is the property of the government of France. I do not need your help now. In fact, m'sieur, I release you from your mission. It is concluded, no? Please leave me now."

Jean-Claude shoved both the rolled document and the diary inside his vest and came to his feet. Longarm had the impression that the idiot marquis intended to defend his find by force of arms if he had to. He—

Rock chips flew off the face of a nearby stone, singing through the air like shrapnel from an artillery burst.

A moment later, Longarm heard the gunshot, but by then he was already on the ground, presenting as low and difficult a target as he could make of himself.

"Get down, Jean-Claude."

"But what . . . ?"

"Mansard, Genevieve, what the hell difference does it make which one of them is shooting at us. Get down out

182

of sight while I scrape the ticks off our backs."

"I do not think. . . ."

"Get *down!*"

Jean-Claude grunted and doubled over. Longarm clearly heard the dull slap of a lead slug hitting red meat. The Frenchman was hit. It remained to be seen how bad it was.

But it sure as hell got him down out of sight. He toppled over, falling onto the clear spot where the cross once was planted and where now there was only an empty, gaping hole in the rock.

"Are you all right?"

"Of course I am not all right, you simpleton. Go shoot someone, will you? You can come back for me when you are done, eh?"

Jean-Claude sounded lively enough. Longarm figured he must not have been hit too badly.

"You got that pistol with you? Keep it handy. Just in case." Longarm rolled onto his side so he could get a better look at the countryside below the mound. He needed to spot the shooter—or shooters—then figure out what he could do about it.

He wished to hell he'd brought the Winchester with him, but it was tucked inside a locked closet back at the hotel with the rest of his gear. When they'd left out of there this morning, he hadn't exactly had this sort of thing in mind.

Not that there was any point in wishing. And he really doubted that the shooter would allow him to run back to the hotel to get his rifle. Unfortunately.

He checked the loads in the single-action Colt he was carrying, and made sure he had some spare cartridges in his coat pocket.

Then he began working his way carefully around the side of the cone so he could get to the back side and begin putting a stalk on whoever it was who was down there throwing lead.

Chapter 39

He heard a gunshot from ground level over on the other
side of the mound, and moments later answering fire, two
shots in quick succession, from Jean-Claude up on top.

A few moments after that, an eddy of breeze carried
the smell of smoke to Longarm, and he smiled just a little.

Jean-Claude was up there wounded and shooting back,
and still was nervy enough to light up a smoke to enjoy
while he waited. Longarm had to concede that the Frenchman really wasn't the useless fop Longarm insisted on
thinking of him as. Jean-Claude had some sand in him
too despite his pickiness and his arrogance.

Even so, Longarm fully intended to see that some
French-speaking representative of the United States of
America got a look at that document Jean-Claude was so
excited about.

As for the gold . . . maybe there really had been some
gold once. Probably had been, in fact. Longarm figured
that would have been stolen and spent long, long ago. The
damned Frenchies likely never cared about that anyway.
It was finding out that those documents still existed that
touched off this hunt. Both hunts, Jean-Claude's and
Louis Mansard's.

Not that any of that was Longarm's worry. All he had to concern himself with now was potting that shooter and getting Jean-Claude and his documents to safety.

He reached the bottom of the mound much quicker and easier than he'd reached the top, and started working his way around to where the shooter had to be.

From up above, Longarm hadn't been able to see the sonuvabitch, and the man had not betrayed himself with a puff of gunsmoke while Longarm happened to be looking. But there was only one spot that Longarm thought would offer enough concealment for an ambush. That was a clump of pale and parched-looking prickly pear that was growing on the sunbaked flat between the Teton mounds and the burning heat of the salt bed.

Longarm eased into a position from which he could see the prickly pear, then waited. Five, six minutes later, he was rewarded with confirmation of his suspicions. There was a thin puff of smoke from the base of the cactus, and soon afterward the sound of a shot.

This time Jean-Claude did not return the fire. But then there was no need.

Longarm took careful aim with the unfamiliar Peacemaker and sent a .45 slug into the spot from which that gunshot came. He followed that with two more, reloaded, and fired three more times, reloaded again.

He hadn't seen anyone run from the prickly pear, and apart from that, there was nothing on the flat growing any taller than ankle high. The shooter had to be in there. But was he—or she—alive? Wounded? Dying? Dead?

The only way to know for sure was to go and look. Longarm was in no hurry to do that. If you have a deer down wounded and bleeding, the worst thing you can do is run up and spook it into running. Give it time to finish dying. That is surer. And in this case, much safer. Longarm returned the Colt to his holster and lighted a brandy crook—damned if he wasn't starting to really like these things—and settled down to wait for a spell.

Longarm waited a full hour, timed by his watch and not estimated, before he stood and made a very cautious approach to the prickly pear.

As it turned out, he needn't have worried. Louis Mansard was there. At least three of Longarm's bullets had found him. He would have survived the one in his hip. He might have survived the one that entered his chest just below the collarbone. There was no way he could have survived the bullet that struck him between the bridge of his nose and his left eye. He had to have been dead from the instant that slug hit him.

Longarm did not regret the wait, though. It beat the hell out of risking being shot by a not-yet-dead adversary.

It pleased the hell out of him to discover that the revolver Mansard used to shoot at them was Longarm's own double-action Colt, taken from him the day the stagecoach was stopped and Jean-Claude was kidnapped.

It felt mighty good to him to have the comfortably familiar gun back in the holster that had been formed to its exact shape.

Longarm cupped his hands and shouted up the slope of the mound, "Hold tight, Jean-Claude. I'm coming to get you."

The climb back up to the top was slow and tiring, but Longarm hurried. He figured he owed Jean-Claude that much.

But again, it turned out that he needn't have been in any rush.

Jean-Claude Gilbert, Marquis de Sant Cerre, was as dead and cold as Louis Mansard. Jean-Claude had been hit in the belly, very much like dying, screaming, agonized Pierre had been.

Jean-Claude had also been hit in his right ear. The

Remington revolver that delivered that killing round was still in his hand.

Jean-Claude had proved at the end to be brave. But not *that* brave. He had seen what Longarm's bullet did to Pierre. He did not want to suffer through that himself to no purpose except to prolong the pain.

Longarm really couldn't blame Jean-Claude for the choice he made.

He rolled the body over, retrieved the leather-bound diary journal from inside Jean-Claude's vest, and reached in again for the sealed and very official-looking document that must surely have been a message to Maximilian.

It was not there.

Longarm looked again.

Then . . . in the pit where the bundle was hidden those long years ago, down where there was protection from the wind, Longarm found ashes and the charred remains of several sulphur matches.

Jean-Claude seemed to have accomplished his mission then. He'd successfully protected his country's secrets. Whatever they may have been.

Longarm would report what Louis Mansard told him. But that proved nothing. France's secrets, whatever they were, were safe now.

Jean-Claude had done well.

Longarm peered off toward the town of Gros Teton. He had the medicine wagon and the roan horse.

He wondered if Genevieve du Charme would like to hitch a ride with him back to wherever the hell he would be going next.

His step was light and his stride long as he headed off to find her and pose that question.

He suspected he knew what her answer would be, he thought with a smile.

Watch for

LONGARM AND THE DEAD MAN'S TALE

300th novel in the exciting LONGARM series from Jove

Coming in November!